# The Black Band

Leis Menachd

Graham Hobbs

First published June 2001

Burcombe Publishing, 1, Burcombe Villas, Chalford
Hill, Stroud, Gloucestershire, GL6 8BN

© Graham Hobbs August 2000.

Pages laid out using Serif Page Plus

Printed by:

Quacks, Jackson House, 7, Grape Lane, Petergate,
York, YO1 7HU

ISBN 0 9519422 2 0

British Library CIP: A catalogue record for this
book is available from the British Library.

# The Black Band

by
Graham Hobbs


Illustrated by


Marling School,
School of the Lion,
Stroud High School,
and
Thomas Keble School

# Places Referred to in this Story

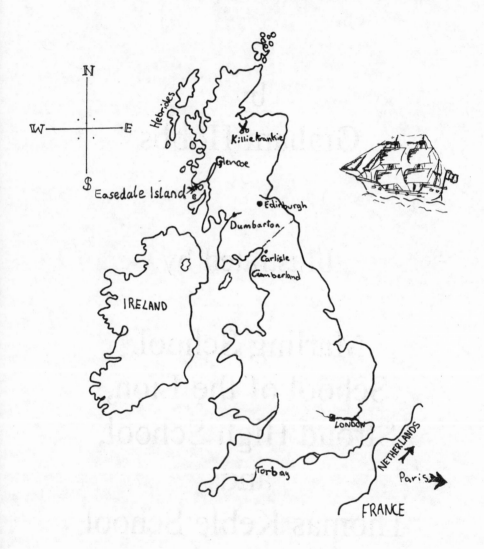

# Background Information

On the 5th of November 1688, an invasion force of 15,000 men led by a Protestant Dutch Prince, William of Orange, landed at Torbay in South Devon. William intended to take control of the throne from his Catholic father-in-law, King James II of England and VII of Scotland. Panic-stricken, James fled to France, allowing the invader and his wife, Mary, to become joint monarchs in his place.

Replacing King James with his daughter and his son-in-law proved very popular in England but it was a very different matter elsewhere. In Scotland and Ireland, James' supporters, who were known as Jacobites, were soon reaching for their swords and resisted the new rulers for decades. They made several attempts to put their man back on the throne and the first of these uprisings forms the background to "The Black Band".

# Notes on language

One of the difficulties of writing a story, set in another country and three centuries ago, is the kind of words to use.

The narrative stays with modern English, making the text more readable and allowing everyday words like "teenager" to appear, even though such words never existed at the time of the story.

However, to keep some of the flavour of the 17th century, the dialogue tends to retain the sort of words people used then. The exception is that obsolete phrases, such as "thou hast", have been avoided where possible, simply to make reading easier.

Purists may object but, to be fair, had this story recorded the exact words of the time and places, Lowlanders would have spoken like Robbie Burns, Lakelanders could have been mistaken for Norwegians and Highlanders would have used Gaelic, an ancient language rarely used outside parts of Scotland. In short, the book would have been unreadable! Nevertheless, to give a feel for this part of Scotland 300 years ago, title pages for each chapter are in both English and Gaelic and footnotes have been used to make some things clearer.

# 1 The Black Band

Bann Dhu

# 1 The Black Band

July 27th 1689

"The sun's gone to bed. Shouldn't you be doing the same?"

Catherine MacDonald's voice interrupted Christina's musings as she sat gazing over Loch Leven.

"I'm coming," she sighed, getting to her feet and turning from the seashore. "I had other things on my mind."

"As usual. What was it this time, a story or a poem? I've never met such a child."

Even as she said it, Catherine realised that "child" was the wrong word to describe Christina these days. The youngster had blossomed into a remarkable teenager, catching the attention of all the young men round about, and most of the older ones too. If only her father hadn't been such a heavy drinker, and so violent at times. There would have been quite a queue of suitors by now and it was easy to see why. Christina was simply beautiful.

Despite being cut short only a few days earlier, her thick black hair still bordered her face in a most attractive manner, a face that featured the loveliest of eyes. They were big and appealing, like a baby's, yet, somewhere behind their dark brown front, they hid a deep, almost mysterious, personality. By contrast, her quaint nose conveyed a cheeky air and when she smiled, you couldn't help but smile back.

Her looks were not her only asset. Like the mother who died giving birth to her, Christina must have been one of the most creative people to have graced the glen. The clothes she made herself were evidence of that, for no one could weave or stitch as neatly as she could and the bright colours she chose were eye-catching to say the least.

"I wasn't feeling poetical," Christina responded as the pair of them made their way along the track, which the sheep had nibbled out of the heather beside the Larroch stream. "I was thinking about my father and the others who've gone to restore King James to his throne."

Catherine, an eternal pessimist with a monotone voice to match, added her own thoughts.

"Aye, it's a sad business when the men go off to fight. There's always fewer come back than go."

"Don't be so miserable," retorted Christina. "Look! It's a beautiful sunset and our men folk are putting the world right. In only a few days they'll all return like heroes, with lots of well-earned plunder, and my father will be amongst them, bringing me home some special souvenir, you'll see."

"All return like heroes? I remember a hero coming home from a raid," mourned Catherine, "wrapped in his plaid* he was, and on the way to his grave on

---

* **Plaid:** Gaelic for blanket. A sheet of tartan wrapped around and belted at the waist to form something like a kilt. The remainder wound over the shoulders.

9

Munda's Isle back there. How can you be sure your father will not be that sort of hero?"

Christina began to feel annoyed.

"Of course everything will be all right. I asked Corrag about it."

Catherine stopped, crossed herself with one hand, seized Christina's arm with the other and swung her around.

"You stupid girl! What were you dealing with her for? She's a witch!"

Christina was taken aback by the old woman's reaction.

"So? Why fret yourself? Lots of people consult her. Anyway, all I did was to ask her how my father could be kept safe and she told me. It was so simple. Do you remember that smart new plaid he wore when he set off, the one I made? Did you notice that extra band in the sett*, you know, the only black one?"

She leaned across and whispered in Catherine's ear.

"Can you keep a secret? That single black band was woven from my own hair. It's charmed. It will give Colin MacColl all the luck and protection he needs."

How little Christina knew. She was already an orphan.

* **Sett:** The layout of coloured bands in a tartan.

# 2 Killiecrankie

## Cille Chreithnich

# 2  Killiekrankie

July 27th 1689

John Clerk leaned on his musket and glared again at the enemy.

"This is ridiculous," he complained. "We cornered them hours ago, we outnumber them two to one and what have we done about it? Just stood here pulling faces at each other."

The old hand on his left gave him a contemptuous look.

"Ridiculous, eh? Wait till you've been in a battle, young man. You'll find that making gestures isn't half as ridiculous as maiming and killing each other. Still, with less than an hour till sunset, let's hope there won't be time and, as for you, be grateful that you'll probably live to see tomorrow."

"He's not cut out to be a soldier," jeered a voice from the rank behind.

"Then why is he standing there in that uniform?" sneered another.

"Because he was fool enough to be taken in by a recruiting officer," replied the first.

John turned to launch into the pair behind him when a shout stopped him midway.

"Silence in the ranks! Heaven help me. When I took up my sword in their Majesties' service, I was promised soldiers to command. That's right, soldiers. And what was I given? You. Yes, you. Call yourselves men? You there!" He was shouting at John. "You're not even facing the right way. Look to your front and if you show your back to the enemy once more I'll make sure you show it to a corporal's whip as well!"

John turned back, silent on the outside but inwardly cursing the two men behind. With their officer once more out of earshot, but not out of sight, they continued to torment John, knowing he wouldn't dare turn on them again.

"So when did Clerk's problems start?"

"When he was born, I'm told."

"Really, as early as that?"

"Oh yes. They say he was a foundling, only a few days old when his mother, or someone, dumped him in the porch of a church. The church was called St. John's and the man who found him was a cleric, so he ended up as John Clerk."

"Give the lad some peace," hissed Patrick O'Shea, the Irishman to John's right. "You'll be glad of his help soon enough when them opposite decide to do anything."

John was grateful for Pat's support, even if the man was an oddity. Most Irish sympathies were with the rebel cause, not the government's, something he never explained. Furthermore, he took nothing seriously and was a constant source of frustration to all who knew him. The trouble was, he had such a disarming charm that few really disliked him. At one time he'd sewn a large white patch, instead of a small red one, over a tear in the arm of his uniform, something no one else would have got away with. Yet even Pat's support wasn't enough for John at that moment. He wished desperately that he could be back in Cumberland, the English lakeland where he'd grown up, and back especially with the slate quarrier he'd been apprenticed to.

Matthew and his wife, Hannah, were a childless couple but John made up for it in some ways. Hannah was a talented cook and an excellent housekeeper, ensuring that John was always well fed and smartly turned out, even to hack away at slates. John should have been grateful. He had a roof over his head and, unusually for an apprentice, a room of his own. These two folk not only cared for him like a son but Matthew even did his best to educate him as well. John was one of the few soldiers who could not only read but write too.

Pat seemed to sense John's thoughts. It was safe to talk again so he asked, "Why didn't you like it in Cumberland?"

"That's simple. My master was too religious. Before he met Hannah, he'd lived in the Scottish Lowlands and his family had been Covenanters - you know, that group that wants a church free of bishops and the like. Well, with time, Matthew reckoned they'd become more political and less spiritual. 'Too ready to use the sword instead of the Bible to win their argument,' was how he put it. It concerned him so much that he crossed the Solway Firth to settle in England. He reckoned that there he could practise his faith more the way he wanted - on me unfortunately." John sighed. "I suppose I

14

was resentful but you can only take so much. What right did he have to inflict his beliefs on his apprentice?"

"You've got a chip on your shoulder about religion, haven't you?"

"Yes, I have." John was in full stream now. "Matthew's supposedly loving God doesn't exist. If He does, why did He put me in the world without a real mother and father? It was too easy for Matthew and Hannah. They had normal parents."

It never occurred to John that it wasn't easy for them. Matthew taught John to read, using the Bible, but John hadn't noticed the tear in Hannah's eye, as they read about another Hannah. The biblical Hannah had been childless too. Neither had it occurred to John that the people he lived with might have been better than his real parents.

"Well, I wasn't having this religious way of life imposed on me," John went on. "I had ideas. I wanted to see other places and do new things. A life of adventure, coupled with lots of money, would do me just right."

"And you thought you'd find it soldiering?"

John looked sheepish.

"Well, no. Something went wrong."

The event was still fresh in John's mind. It was his first visit over the border to Scotland. Matthew was visiting his cousin Andrew, in Dumbarton, and had taken John with him for company. Disobeying Matthew, John had slipped into a tavern one day, to sulk over a drink.

"Hallo my lad!" greeted a friendly man in uniform. "It's a bit crowded in here and you have the only spare places at your table. Would you mind if my sergeant and I joined you? You look a bit glum and I'm sure we could cheer you up!"

John couldn't see any reason to refuse and gestured to the chair with his hand.

"Thank you kindly, young man. Landlord! Bring a flagon of my usual for my friend here."

The drinks appeared. John had no idea what the "usual" was but it turned out to be quite powerful. The new arrivals began to talk to him about the great life they'd had in the army, the places they'd visited and the heroic deeds they'd witnessed, not to mention performed, themselves.

"Before I took my officer's advice and joined up, I'd been a badly paid farm labourer," stated the sergeant. "Not now, though. He makes sure that the men of his company have a regular wage and everybody admires us in our smart uniforms, especially the pretty ladies. Isn't that right, sir?"

The sergeant winked as he stressed the bit about the ladies and the officer grinned back but John hadn't noticed. He was soaking up the talk, as well as another couple of drinks, and beginning to think this could be what he was looking for. His new companions encouraged him.

"Aye, Sergeant, I do believe that if we'd had more of our friend's sort from the start, we'd have beaten the French years ago. Instead, we're still fighting them now. Just look at those fine muscles! I've no doubt he has a fine character to match, too."

Helped by the alcohol, John was in a dream. He could see it all, a magnificent uniform, money in his pocket, a cheering crowd and much more. It was too much and he left with, or rather was helped off by, the other two.

His thoughts moved from the tavern, back to the front of the government army, as they stood facing the rebels.

"Joining this regiment was the biggest mistake of my life," he said bitterly. "I've never been paid and I can see why. The more of us that get killed, the less back pay they have to cough up. Still, they'll be disappointed, won't they? The light's fading and there's the command to stand down."

The ranks of red uniforms began to disperse. Most of the men were relieved that they hadn't come to grips with the rebels but it was short-lived. This dispersal was exactly what the Earl of Dundee, commander of the force opposite, had been waiting for. With terrifying shouts and screams, the Highlanders launched themselves down on their enemies. Total confusion broke out in General MacKay's forces, as they tried to regroup and stop the oncoming wave.

John's memories of the next few moments were hazy. He remembered an arrow hitting Pat square in the middle of the white patch on his arm, causing the Irishman to drop his musket and produce a mass of Irish bad language. There was a command to fire and in the following second several hundred

17

Highland wives became widows. Not that it stopped the charge. Hundreds of survivors swarmed on, down the slope. There were shouts from government officers of "Fix bayonets!" and "Stand firm!" but they meant nothing to John. He simply stood staring at his weapon.

"It didn't fire, Pat. It didn't fire! What am I going to do?"

Pat's response was to turn and run. "Come on, boy," he called over his shoulder. "This is a good time to leave."

# 3 Freedom

*Saorsa*

# 3 Freedom

July 27th 1689

A few infantrymen were still fumbling to fix bayonets into the muzzles of their guns as the wild charge hit them, though John missed that part. He had joined the bulk of the army, those who were fleeing the field.

Less than a minute after the enemy had begun their charge, they'd passed beyond where John and the others had been stationed and were chasing them across the countryside. A complete rout was narrowly averted thanks to the government general and what few professional soldiers he could rally. He made them stand their ground long enough to take the momentum out of the Highland charge, enabling him to withdraw the remnant of the army from the field. Not that there was much left to withdraw. Most of his soldiers had deserted at the first opportunity and, no matter how gallantly he'd fought himself, Hugh MacKay had lost one of the shortest battles in British history.

Such matters meant nothing to John as he pounded after the figure of Pat, who was hurrying over the short rise ahead. As Pat veered away from the main body of men, and turned along a small wooded ravine, John followed and soon caught up with him.

"This way," wheezed Pat, as he scuttled up the

side of the ravine, to hide amongst the vegetation. "Right," he panted, "let's lie low here until I get my breath back. You know, I really am getting too old for this sort of thing." He paused for a minute before continuing. "Well, lad, I'm after thinking as we're out of it and safe for the moment."

"I'm not sure of that," doubted John. "Why did we have to come here, instead of staying with the others? There's safety in numbers and we're on our own now."

"Not at all, young man. Firstly, *we* didn't have to come here. It was my idea and you chose to follow. Secondly, there's safety in numbers you say? And just who might those gentlemen in their many-coloured skirts be pursuing at this very moment? The bulk of the army, not us. Anyway, even if we were still in those poor fools' company, how many of them would stop and help us if we got into mischief? None of them. I somehow had the impression that it was every man for himself back there."

"Maybe so, but the rebels weren't all chasing after the men we separated from. I saw several who'd given up the chase and they're probably looking for us now."

Pat was preoccupied with extracting the arrow from his arm but he managed to keep the argument on the boil.

"They are not. Them ones as stopped did so because they'd found the baggage train. By now they'll be too busy looting to bother us. No, slipping up here was a good move, believe me, a good move."

Pat slipped his coat off and rolled his sleeve up before continuing.

"Here, while you're waiting, wrap this piece of material around my wound. I can't reach to do it properly. Gently now, you'll make it worse!"

John did as he was told while the Irishman carried on with his chatter.

"An arrow!" he continued. "Here's us with guns routed by savages with primitive bows and arrows. I'm not sure whether to keep this as a souvenir or break it up in contempt."

"I'd save it," grinned John. "Find yourself a bow and you can send it back! Let's face it, you may call the thing primitive but it works. After all, how many arrows can a man loose in a minute? Half a dozen? It takes some of us that long to fire and reload once and my weapon," he kicked the matchlock beside him, "didn't even go off."

"Maybe," mused Pat, as John added a final knot to his handiwork. "Still, that's history now. Seeing as you've finished playing the surgeon and all the fuss has died down, we'd best be off. It'll mean a detour but we should be back among our own side by morning. They'll have regrouped a few miles over that way." He nodded in the direction he meant.

"In that case I'm all for going another way. I don't want anything more to do with soldiering."

"Really? So where might you be heading instead?"

"Anywhere, so long as it doesn't involve any more fighting."

Pat paused for effect before innocently asking, "And, er, how far were you planning on travelling in that uniform?"

John looked down at his bright red coat. Talk about a dead give-away. He had no clear answer but he was still determined to be out of things.

"At this moment, I don't care. Just look after yourself and your wound because I'm off."

"You'll be back when you realise I'm right," Pat called after him. "I'll give you thirty minutes to change your mind and then I'm off too."

John didn't reply but just carried on. Pat sat back, filled his pipe with tobacco and lit it. He had a smug look on his face as he waited for John to return, admitting that Pat was right after all. A full twenty minutes passed before Pat, who'd been toying with the arrow and thinking up a good yarn to go with it, began to wonder if John really had gone off by himself. Then he saw the figure of John hurrying back.

"I knew you'd see it my way. Now if you'd taken my advice in the first place ..."

A clearly shaken John interrupted Pat's flow and seized his arms.

"I've just killed someone. I think I'm going to be sick!"

This wasn't quite the reunion Pat expected. He winced and shrugged his arms free of John's grip.

"That's a fine thing to do."

"What's so fine about killing someone? He's dead, I know it."

"I wasn't referring to that little incident. Don't you realise that you grabbed my wound? One minute you're tending it and the next you're opening it up again. It's a good thing I took the arrow out first. Now what's your problem?"

"I've killed someone. He just jumped out at me, swinging a sword, and I instinctively swung back at him with my musket. The stock* caught him square on the side of his head. It made a horrid noise and I'm going to be sick."

Pat grabbed the musket. "Here, give me that. Sure, you'll hurt someone with it if you're not careful. Right, now pass me your bayonet."

"Why can't you use your own?"

Pat sighed at the fool in front of him. "Because I need it to protect myself, idiot."

"What about me?"

"Sure you can protect me as well. Now just give me your bayonet."

Yet again, John gave up trying to follow Pat's logic and passed him the weapon. Pat fixed it into the barrel and peered around before edging forward.

"Show me where it happened. Go carefully too. The light's almost gone but there may still be others around."

John led him to the edge of the woodland, where his victim could be plainly seen sprawled across the ground. Pat held the bayonet to the prostrate Highlander's back and lifted the musket to strike home.

*Stock: The wooden butt or handle on a gun.

24

"No! Don't do that," begged John, pushing Pat aside.

"If you thump my wounded arm once more, sure and I'll poke this bayonet through the corresponding part of your own anatomy and you'll know what it feels like."

"Don't kill him. I think I'm going to be sick."

This being the third time John had talked about being sick, Pat moved over just in case he meant it.

"I'll never understand the logic of you English. If the man is as dead as you say, why can't I kill him as well?"

"Because he might not be dead after all."

"Precisely. So if I kill him too there's no chance of him doing us any more harm is there? Look, he tried to kill you and you're giving him the opportunity of doing it again."

"Please! I think I'm ..."

"I know, you're going to be sick. Well go over there and do it. I'll deal with this."

John returned a few minutes later. "Is he ... ? Did you ... ?"

"Yes he is so I didn't have to. Mind you he stinks of whisky. He must have been so drunk that it's not surprising that he failed to hit you and didn't get out the way when you retaliated. But we've delayed enough. If you two hadn't carried on the battle after it was supposed to be finished, we could have been away by now. Are you coming?"

"No. I told you I'm not. I'll take my chances elsewhere, even in this uniform."

"Hmm," mused Pat. "Have it your way but, before you go, you might be interested in a fine thought as I've had. You know, you don't have to be in that uniform."

"No? So what else am I supposed to wear?"

Pat kicked the casualty. "How about his clothes? Sure, he'll not be needing them himself, will he?"

"That's awful!"

"Is it? Listen. As I see it, you have three choices. First, you can take your chances with me, with my string of tried and proven excuses which will keep us out of trouble when we rejoin our regiment. Second, you can ditch your uniform and, in this Highlander's clothes, you could get by with no problem at all. Just avoid meeting any of our side or theirs. Lastly, you can wander off just as you are, though I seem to recall as the last time you did that, you didn't get very far. They don't take prisoners, you know."

John felt dubious but considered his former adversary and what he was wearing. It was simple enough, little more than a large sheet, belted at the waist with the rest wrapped around the chest and shoulders.

"Very well," John conceded. "Give me a hand."

"I knew you'd see reason in the end," said Pat, pulling the body under the cover of the trees while John discarded his coat, shoes and breeches. In no time he was wrapped in his new attire.

"And a fine figure you cut too," complimented Pat, even though it was hardly light enough to see by

26

now. "But before you depart, I'd appreciate keeping this gun. I'm sure it was mine you must have picked up by accident and I'd also be glad of this sword which the gentleman used to introduce himself to you. I'll be needing the gun, you see, to prove as I didn't drop it and run away. Also I'll be needing the sword as evidence that I've been in action and done my duty by killing one of their majesties' enemies."

"And what am I to take care of myself with?"

"Here, I'll let you have the bayonet from my weapon. It's no trouble for I'm wearing a spare of my own. It's a very versatile and convenient tool, a bayonet. It'll be everything you'll be wanting of it."

John considered his situation. A musket would be heavy on a long journey and, if he was found with it in his possession, he'd have some explaining to do. As to the sword, he wasn't so sure but, once again, Pat got the better part of the bargain as John swapped the sword in order to get his own bayonet back.

"What about this man? We can't leave him here."

"True. It might raise some suspicions."

"No, I mean shouldn't he be laid to rest properly?" Pat sighed, crossed himself and kicked the body so that it rolled into the undergrowth before ending with, "Amen."

"What sort of funeral was that?"

"A better one than most of the others lying on the field will be getting. Meanwhile, you interrupted the full military honours I was going to give to the departed by adding these."

He threw John's coat and breeches after the body. "There. Oh, I nearly forgot. These too."

"Not my shoes! I've a lot of miles to cover!"

"Sorry, it must be your shoes and all. Have you ever seen a Highlander wearing army footwear instead of being barefoot? Well, we've delayed long enough. Have a safe journey, John. I'll tell them that I saw you gallantly fall in the line of duty but not before you shot one man, bayoneted two more and clubbed a third. Shame about your pay arrears."

With that he was gone. John waited a moment, said his own silent prayer about the dead man, not that it made him feel any better, and slipped off.

Because of the dark and the continual need for caution, he only travelled four miles in the few hours before dawn. It was a dawn which found him hungry and lost but he didn't care. Instead, he sat and watched the sunrise, soaking up the picture as the light grew.

"Shame about my pay arrears indeed! Look at that sunrise. It's a sight I might never have seen again and how much back pay is that worth, Patrick O'Shea? I'm free. Free! I'm not a prisoner of the rebels, nor a prisoner of my own side either. The army no longer owns me. As far as they are concerned, Private Sentinel John Clerk died at the Battle of Killiecrankie."

# 4 The Traveller

*Fear Siubhail*

# 4 The Traveller

July 28th 1689

Cheered by his new circumstances, John thought about the future. He was hundreds of miles from home and in a hostile country but he wasn't worried. He had a simple plan to get out of the situation. Each day, he would note where the sun rose and then look in exactly the opposite direction. If the sun rose in the east, the opposite direction must be west. He would fix his sights on a westerly point and head for it. Sooner or later he would reach the west coast.

There, he intended to turn south. Scotland didn't go on forever. Sooner or later, the west coast of Scotland had to become the west coast of England and that meant Cumberland and home.

It seemed odd to think of Matthew and Hannah's house as home now but that was how it felt. He didn't yet realise that he faced a journey of around 200 miles and that he was heading deeper into the rebel homelands. His mind was on other problems.

He'd already solved one of them, the weather, now that he was getting the hang of his new attire. Until he'd had to wear it, he hadn't realised how practical such simple clothing could be. It was comfortable, fitted any size of person and the choice of colours made an excellent camouflage. On top of that, it was so versatile. When he felt cold, he wrapped the plaid around both his shoulders, instead of just one. When it looked like rain, he simply slid the part which lay around his neck up and over his head, just like a hood. At night he could unbelt and remove the cloth, then roll himself up in it, to make a primitive sleeping bag. He wasn't so happy about his bare feet but there wasn't much he could do about that.

Unfortunately, new problems began to emerge, ones that were less easy to deal with. For a start, John couldn't approach anybody. If he came across his own side, dressed the way he was, he could be mistaken for an enemy. Conversely, if he came across any of the locals he'd be in trouble with them too, the moment they found out that he couldn't speak their language. There was nothing for it. He would just have to be content with his own company.

However, being on his own created further problems. How was he going to eat, for one? John didn't realise until then how much he depended on other people for food. It looked like he would have to live off the land. Bleak though it appeared, it ought to provide him with something, wild or stolen.

"Then what do I do about cooking it?" thought John. "I've nothing to light a fire with and, even if I had, I risk the smoke giving me away. It looks like no company and raw food. Oh well, best get on with it." With that he set off.

By the end of the day, he had travelled less than ten miles. It wasn't far and he had no load to carry, yet he felt exhausted. Trying to travel barefoot and without being seen was slow work. He was desperately hungry too. He'd tried approaching a remote building, to see what he could steal, but he'd failed. Whilst he was still some distance away, two collie-like dogs had noticed his approach and chased noisily after him. Fortunately no one had followed. That evening he sat miserably on the wooded slope above the northern shore of Loch Tummel. He'd eaten after a fashion - a fish he'd trapped in a stream. He didn't even know what sort it was and it had to be eaten raw. Still, people do that sort of thing when they are hungry.

The next evening saw the fugitive a dozen miles further, on the south side of Loch Rannoch. He'd travelled a little further that day because he was getting less careful. Now he was in Coille Dubh, the Black Wood of Rannoch. The pine trees edging the loch, with its beach of red garnets, made a beautiful picture, though at that moment John was in no mood for admiring the scenery. His hunger was making him weak and light-headed.

It was then that he heard a splash to his left, and saw a figure swimming out in the loch. As he watched, John had a very tempting thought. People tend to leave things on the shore when they go swimming and why should this one be any different? It was a bit of a long shot, but the swimmer might even have left some food somewhere. What was there to lose by looking?

The person in the water was enjoying his swim and didn't notice John sidling through the trees and bracken until, just in front of him was what he was looking for.

A full set of clothes, the style John was more used to seeing, lay neatly folded in the heather and next

32

to them were a pair of well-made polished leather boots. John looked just a few inches beyond the footwear and stared hopefully at a saddlebag. Nearby stood the horse that normally carried it. At that moment it was happily munching some vegetation.

John reached forward and was delighted to find he could clutch the bag. The horse turned and looked inquisitively in John's direction.

"Good boy. Don't make a sound," pleaded John.

The horse obviously wasn't worried and it remained quiet as John nervously opened the bag and found what he craved - food. Ravenous though he'd become, he decided not to eat straightaway. He grabbed a loaf of bread and some cheese before considering what to do with a tempting bottle of wine. He compromised. He drew out the cork, took two swigs and put it back.

John was about to depart when the clothes gave him a further idea. He'd have to change his own at some stage. This might be the time. Although the swimmer had been in the cold water for at least ten minutes, he was still enjoying his bathe and had even moved further from the shore. That settled it.

The horse still stared passively as John, on the other side of the branches, cast aside the plaid and hastily drew the other clothes through to his side of the branches. They were the finest clothes he'd seen in a long time but he threw them on sloppily without even doing up the buttons. He wanted to be away as fast as he could. But then he stopped for a moment.

His conscience was troubling him again. It had been bad enough with the previous person and, as Pat had said, he hadn't needed his clothes anymore but this time it was different. Matthew had drummed it into John not to steal and this was definitely stealing. Maybe an exchange wouldn't be so bad. To feel a bit less guilty, John neatly folded up his plaid and passed it through to where the other man's clothes had once been. There, he felt a bit less of a robber now.

Just before quitting the scene, he took a final look at the horse. One of those might come in useful ... No, on second thoughts, that really would be pushing his luck too far. John put his finger across his mouth and winked at the horse. The animal continued to stare silently as the thief made off as fast as he could.

Well away from the scene, and hidden with his ill-gotten gains, John munched his bread and cheese. He missed seeing the expression on the swimmer's face when he came ashore. The man was a Highlander but there were times when it suited him to wear lowland clothes. Now, his most expensive ones were gone and he was naturally angry. He had nothing left for the time being except his horse, a stranger's plaid and some scraps of food. He examined the plaid. The cloth was quite new and well made, which was some consolation. He began fitting it round himself, but hesitated. There was something odd about the sett. It had a solitary black band running through it.

# 5 The Rescue

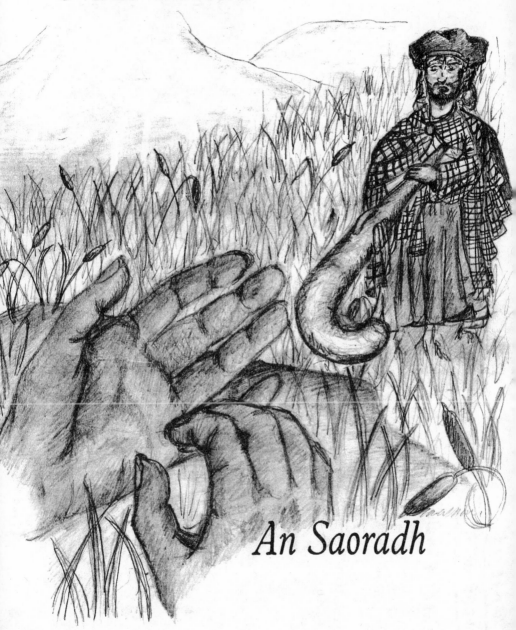

*An Saoradh*

# Features of Glencoe area.

## Scale: 1 inch = 3 miles.

Fort William (drove road)

Kinlochleven

Devils Staircase

Aonach Eagach Ridge

Rannoch Moor

Great Shepherd of Etive

Glen Etive

Little Shepherd of Etive

Three Sisters

Loch Achtriochtan

R. Coe

Loch Leven

Glencoe Village

munda's Isle

Ballachulish

R. Laroch

Ballachulish Ferry

Bidean nam Bian (Pinnacle of Peaks)

Fort William (coast road)

N  E  W  S

# 5 The Rescue

August the 1st 1689

The smoke from the smouldering peat fires drifted slowly in the evening air. This year, far fewer of the Glencoe folk had moved up to their summer settlement on Rannoch Moor. Most of the men were busy elsewhere, chasing redcoats, settling old scores with rival clans and generally picking up booty. They were in their element.

The dependants they had left behind were reasonably safe in Glencoe itself. The name means "Narrow Glen," and for centuries the people in it had felt themselves immune to the attention of rival clans and even the king and government. Their natural fortress was protected to the north by the Aonach Eagach Ridge, whose sheer, almost unclimbable crags, reached skywards for more than 3,000 feet. To the south was a range of mountain spurs spreading out from Bidean nam Bian, the highest mountain in Argyllshire. Few people crossed that range, even in the best of weather. There were only two viable entrances, from Loch Leven in the west and Rannoch Moor in the east. Both were easily guarded.

Some women, children and a few men over sixty, folk whose age or gender excluded them from fighting, had taken the variety of animals they had for summer grazing on the moor. It was something of a risk for, beyond the safety of their glen and without more able-bodied men around, they and their animals made easy and tempting targets for raiders, especially here. Rannoch Moor was known to harbour outlaws from clan Gregor.

Donald and his granddaughter, Christina, were among those who'd moved, together with their two shaggy black calves and half a dozen sheep. It was better grazing on the moor because the glen couldn't support all the livestock. They also reasoned that they should be safe this year because most of the troublemakers would be on the same side at that moment and fighting miles away.

On top of that, Donald was a Glencoe man. Nobody threatened him and got away with it. At least, that's what he told his neighbours but, being a practical man, he had his gun along with him too. It was probably the only one left, for the younger men had taken almost every kind of weapon they could find to the rebellion. For good measure, Donald also had Fingal, the large deer-hound, with him. At over a yard high at the shoulder and weighing more than Donald himself, the dog was purely for company of course.

Christina had been gathering the animals together for the evening, when Fingal bolted after a hare. He was trained to leave domestic animals alone but anything else was fair game. In fact he had to hunt such things because his owner rarely fed him. Colin, Christina's father, reckoned that a dog that had to catch his own dinner made a better hunter.

Christina ignored the dog and concentrated on moving the other animals, when she heard a distant howl. She instantly recognised it and knew that Fingal had got himself into trouble. Calling for her grandfather to follow, she headed off in the direction of the noise. The hare had led the hound on a fast chase for half a mile across the moor, until Fingal had floundered in a mire. The poor dog struggled to get out but found himself sinking even more. By the time Christina appeared only his neck, head and front paws were visible.

Christina had no idea what to do. She daren't try to get close, for fear of sinking herself. Then a stranger appeared on the scene. He'd also heard the dog's cry and had come to see what was wrong.

Christina appealed to him to help but he didn't seem to understand. Nevertheless, he seemed to have the same concern, for he tried to approach the trapped animal. Unfortunately, he only had to step forward a foot before he sank twice as many. This was no good. He stopped, frowned and shook his head. Christina noted the reluctance on his face as he removed his magnificent coat and spread it out ahead of him, right up to all that still showed of Fingal, his head.

The man crawled on his belly across the coat, which started to give way. He just managed to reach the scruff of the dog's neck and pull. It made the dog come up and forwards slightly but the coat sank ominously. Christina shouted encouragement but the newcomer ignored her and eased himself back a fraction. He pulled again and, though the dog came nearer, the coat sank much further.

There was terror in the animal's eyes but he seemed to understand what was happening and his front paws reappeared to help him pull forward.

"Come on. You can do it. Pull, Fingal! Pull!" shouted Christina.

Fingal got a grip on the edge of the coat and gave a heave. He got himself much higher, climbed over his rescuer and reached the solid ground. Christina gaped in horror as the dog trod the man down into the mire. The man struggled and turned himself over, gasping for breath. His coat had completely disappeared and he was following it.

It was a cruel minute as the rescuer now tried to rescue himself. Christina jumped up and down and shouted advice to him but she was next to useless. She watched as the man pushed on the submerged coat to ease himself up. The trouble was that the coat sank even further into the depths as he did so. It was a fine balancing act.

"God, please get me out of this. Please!" he cried.

Christina didn't understand what he said but

prayed a similar prayer for him in her own tongue.

Then Donald appeared with his gun. The sinking figure watched for what seemed an eternity as Christina and Donald waved their arms about and shouted nineteen to the dozen at each other, before they came to some agreement. Then Donald stepped forward as far as he dared. Christina held his left hand to anchor him, while he used his right to hold out the barrel of his gun. It didn't reach.

"Do something! I'm drowning!" wailed the man.

Donald and Christina didn't understand and had no other ideas but fortunately more capable neighbours began to turn up to see what the excitement was all about. One carried the answer, a shepherd's crook. Longer than a gun and with a hooked end, he easily managed to reach the outstretched hands with it. Even then, it took the efforts of two men to haul the man to solid ground, where other willing hands grasped his arms and helped pull him clear.

Neither party understood each other but the rescued man took the shepherd's hand in both of his and grasped it tightly. The shepherd was embarrassed and turned to speak to one of the spectators. The man he talked to spoke some English.

"How are you?" he asked.

"Wet and cold but glad to be alive," answered the newcomer. "Please thank this man for me."

The English speaker turned and translated the reply. The whole group seemed to approve and patted the man with the crook on his back. Then Donald, having finished checking over his son's dog, spoke to the interpreter who nodded and faced the peat-encrusted man again.

"I am Hector MacDonald. This gentleman is Donald MacColl," he explained. "He and his granddaughter, Christina, thank you for saving their dog. They ask you to have some food with them and stay for the night. Who are you and what do you say?"

"My name is John Clerk and I would be grateful," he said.

John looked at the smiling faces as they heard his answer translated. He didn't feel like smiling himself. He'd lost a decent coat, along with three sovereigns he'd been delighted to find in the pocket. Worst of all, he'd nearly drowned, all because of a stupid dog. Was it worth it? He scanned the faces around him and, now that he wasn't struggling for his life, he had time to pay proper attention to his new hostess. Her big brown eyes beamed with admiration.

"Mmm," he thought, "perhaps it was worth it!"

# 6 Living with the Enemy

## A Fuireachd Leis An Namhàid

# 6 Living with the Enemy

August 2nd 1689

John was awoken by Hector. Christina was in the background with a steaming bowl.

"You slept much, Master Clerk," said Hector, enjoying showing off his ability to speak English, "but now it is time to enjoy the sun and some food."

John came out of the primitive shelter he'd shared with Donald, expressed his appreciation and took the wooden bowl. Hector, Christina and Donald sat opposite and, though Christina appeared to be busy with her spindle, John was aware that she was watching him whenever she felt it safe to do so. She needed a bit more practice, for John looked up at one point and caught her studying him. She hastily looked away, leaving John slightly embarrassed but secretly pleased. Christina tried to cover her slip by asking Hector something. Hector turned to John.

"Christina would like to know where you will go from here and when you want to leave. Can she and her grandfather help you on your journey?"

They all wanted to know what brought this foreigner to these parts at such an unlikely time but Highland hospitality forbade offending guests. For his part John was relieved not to have to give explanations and decided to keep as close to the truth as he could.

"I want to go to the sea, head south and return to England," said John through his porridge.

Hector didn't translate straight away but frowned

and rubbed his fingers over his grey bearded chin. He always did that when he was thinking. Finally he spoke.

"That's a walk of many days, weeks perhaps," he informed John. "You would do better to take a boat."

"I would have to work my passage if I did that," commented John as he licked his bowl clean. "The only money I had to pay my fare was in my coat pocket and that is now at the bottom of a bog."

His tone brightened as Christina piled some more porridge into his bowl.

"Ooh, thanks," he said.

Christina acknowledged John's words with a sheepish smile, hoping that "Ooh, thanks" was English for something like "You are a brilliant cook and, in the eyes of all men, you are the most stunning woman to walk the earth." Sadly, she suspected it didn't mean that. Meanwhile, John was too busy tucking into the second bowl of food to notice anyone, let alone what they might be thinking. He was clearly hungry and probably lost and Hector felt some sympathy for him.

"Perhaps I can help you," he eventually suggested. "I myself have a boat, not a big one, but it serves me well enough. After my son, Angus, returns from his patriotic duty, serving King James, if we have cause to sail south ourselves, we could take you with us, as far as we go.

"Hector, you are a gentleman," replied John. "Here's my hand on it. Meanwhile, this porridge really is the best I've ever tasted. How do I say to

45

Christina, 'Thank you for the porridge and is there any more?'"

"I'll do it," said Hector, before passing on John's request direct to Christina.

"He's eaten up yours, Grandfather's, and my porridge already!" she responded. "And when do I get an answer to my question and why were you shaking hands?"

As Hector explained everything, John noticed that Christina's lovely face took on a sad look. Hector didn't see it and addressed John again.

"I don't think Angus and the others will be away for long. Perhaps they will be back in September."

"Next month? What do I do for the next few weeks?"

"Eat up all we have," thought Hector to himself before consulting Donald. Before Donald could answer Christina tugged on his arm and talked in an animated way to her grandfather. He appeared a little uncertain but then he shrugged his shoulders and seemed to agree. Christina looked relieved as Hector faced John again.

"Donald would count it a great honour if you would be his guest until we can take you home."

John weighed up the situation. Would an unknown language and cramped sleeping conditions be worth Christina's company? He glanced at her. She returned him the same look as she'd given him the night before and scored a hit.

"The honour would be mine," he said.

John spent the rest of that day usefully cutting

peat for Donald. He helped other folk with any activities which required a bit of muscle and they appreciated him for it. At the end of the day, he was tired out but popular. He slept soundly.

On day two, he took a break from work and played shinty with the youngsters. It was a primitive game, without a proper playing field. The patches of bog and heather made interesting obstacles and there seemed to be no limit to the size of the pitch. No one seemed too clear what the rules were either. Even assaulting the other side with your stick seemed to be acceptable every so often. John was the oldest player, but he regularly allowed himself to be beaten (in both senses of the word) if it helped the losing side. His popularity grew further.

One activity which impressed him was when he joined in a hunt with the few men and the two deer hounds still around. Fingal and Fraoch were considered too old to go off with the fighters but they were still brilliant at their work. They scented a herd of red deer, separated one of them from the rest, cornered it and brought it down before meekly giving it up to the men. All that needed doing was to dress the carcass, reward the dogs with some scraps and carry the dinner home. The dogs had done virtually everything else. The venison was enjoyed around a camp fire as the whole community got together for some stories, singing and occasional dancing. John was making friends and lapping up the culture. He almost forgot the passing of time.

Well into September, he had begun to grasp

Gaelic speech as well. One of the best ways to learn another language is to live among the people who use it, as John did. He could have used Hector as an interpreter but he preferred to try listening to the words and practising them for himself. This was mainly so that he could talk to Christina, with whom he was now well and truly smitten. She was his teacher most of the time and she used a simple technique. He pointed to things and she told him the names. For revision Christina would point and John had to say the word.

From nouns, or names of things, they moved on to adjectives, or descriptive words. John learned to count and then went on to colours and sizes. The test that followed this exercise was for Christina to give John a word and he would describe whatever it was.

By now it was getting confusing because, in other languages, people say their words in a different order. Gaelic also has genders and cases. If anyone reading this hasn't come across such things, don't worry. Just be grateful.

John was finding learning this new language frustrating but he was so infatuated by his teacher that he kept at it. Fortunately, Christina couldn't read, so he was spared the very different Gaelic spelling.

John wished these weeks could have gone on for ever, but life is never constant. Everything changed one autumnal morning when an excited youngster came running back with news from the moor.

"The men are coming home!"

# 7 The Return of the Warriors

## Tilleadh Na Gaisgeach

# 7 The Return of the Warriors

September 1689

Excitement spread as people heard that the men were returning from their escapades. There was an air of expectancy, though it was tinged with anxiety too. John watched as they arrived.

At the front was a tall proud man on a pony. His fierce face sported what people today would call a "handlebar" moustache. It reached right round to the thick mane of white hair which flowed down his back. He wore a leather jacket and trews*. Behind him came his gillies** and a piper.

"He must be MacIain, the chief," John guessed correctly.

The rest of the little army was spread out. Some looked proud, like their leader, others disheartened. Several had clearly been wounded and were being helped by their comrades. Those who could carried their weapons, and much booty besides. In the distance some could be seen herding cattle, sheep and horses. They'd robbed a lot of people on the way home, though they wouldn't have called it that. To them it was "collecting their wages."

At first the spectators cheered but then folk started to run along the line of men, looking for loved ones or news of them. Some found what they were looking for and embraced fathers, husbands and sons, delighted too, by their "souvenirs".

* **Trews:** Tartan trousers. ** **Gillies:** Personal attendants

One man presented his wife with a copper pan. Another put a ring on his sweetheart's finger. A third laid a beautiful shawl round his mother's shoulders. One fellow picked up his son, who could not have been more than six years old, and carried him high on his shoulders while the youngster struggled to wave a heavy sword that had once belonged to a Government officer. John stared, impressed with the men's thoughtful generosity. He hadn't realised yet that none of it was paid for.

Most of the welcoming party felt relief at finding their breadwinners alive, although the wounds some had suffered naturally caused concern. A few, however, grew more and more anxious at not finding who they were looking for and lots of wailing began as they found out the truth.

Despite John's progress with the language, there was so much noise and gabbling that he understood very little. He wandered to the rear of the party to look at the animals, which the last few men were driving along.

Hector was already there, leading a massive plough horse whose short rider looked out of place.

"Ah, there you are, John," greeted Hector. "Meet my son, Angus. He speaks English."

Short Angus looked down from his tall perch. "Good day, John. Excuse me sitting up here but I cannot walk easily." He pointed to his bandaged shin. "Musket ball," he explained.

John looked at this small but dignified and well-spoken youth. Surely he couldn't have been one

51

of the savages who had charged after him at Killiecrankie? Apparently he was. As Hector listened, Angus brought John up to date.

"I suppose you heard the news. We won a spectacular victory at Killiecrankie. You should have been there, John. Did you know, we Glencoe men were the first to reach and loot the enemy baggage train? Yes, we were. I've brought a surprise for my father and lots more besides."

He hesitated, then continued in a more sombre vein. "I wish it could have continued like that but, once we counted our losses, our excitement was short-lived. Bonnie Dundee, our leader, was killed too, shot right at the moment of victory. That's when things began to turn sour. There will never be another commander like him. Some clans gave up and returned home but we stuck with the cause and went on to attack Perth.

"We only got as far as Dunkeld. We were brave fighters but badly led. They placed us in exposed fields, facing an enemy sheltered behind barricades in the town. I got this hole in my leg and missed the hand-to-hand fighting through the streets. I was fortunate. The attack got bogged down and eventually all we could do was withdraw."

Angus paused. He'd used the word "withdraw" because he knew enough English to realise that it didn't sound as bad as "retreat," but it still stuck in his throat. He carried on more slowly.

"I was carried from the battlefield by my cousin. That evening, the chiefs had a council of war. They decided that we had done all we could for this year and we went our separate ways. It was a feeble end to what began so well."

Angus tried to put a brave face on things but John felt sure his voice was wavering as he tried to finish his tale.

"Still, we gave the Glenlyon Campbells something to remember us by on the way home. They were a bit reluctant but we persuaded them to pay us some of our wages. This used to be one of their horses. I suppose it's some compensation for our losses."

Tears began to well up in Angus' eyes as he tried to hold his composure.

"We left here three months ago with over a hundred men. We've returned with more than thirty lost and no end of wounded. We've paid dearly for all this plunder."

With that, the tears overflowed. Hector tried to comfort his son with soothing words but John had no idea what to say. He simply patted Angus on his thigh and walked off, leaving him to his mourning.

By the time he arrived back at the primitive settlement, John found a changed population. Some had gone on with their men folk and their new possessions, down to their regular homes in the glen itself. Others were staying for a day or so longer. Christina was still there, sitting with her head in Catherine's lap. Her shawl was across her face and Catherine's arm was around her quivering shoulder. As Catherine noticed him, John felt like an intruder. Catherine seemed to feel the same and waved him off but it had the wrong effect. Christina sensed the movement and looked up. Instinctively, she ran and threw her arms around the new man in her life. John was so taken aback that he didn't know what to do. He remained still as she sobbed into his shoulder.

*"Tha m'-athair marbh!"*

He only understood "It is" and "my" but he guessed the rest and it made him angry. Wars were indescribably stupid. Less than two months ago John would have seen it as his duty to run a bayonet through Angus. Today, after meeting him for only a few minutes, John saw him, not as an enemy, but as somebody he liked. Yet the poor lad could no longer walk properly. What was the point? On top of that, a lot of peaceful folk had been robbed to pay these men, inviting retribution and leading to further bloodshed. Worst of all, Christina was devastated by the loss of her father.

John lifted her chin. A silk handkerchief had survived the incident in the bog and, apart from washing it out, he'd kept it neatly tucked away. It had seemed too good to use for anything, till now. Gently, he wiped Christina's tears and spoke softly.

"I'm sorry you can't understand me in English but it's the only way I can find the words. I want to tell you that I love you. To see you hurt, hurts me. I'm incensed by what's happened and it's a good thing that whoever killed your father isn't around now. I'd make him suffer for it!"

# 8 Gold from Slate

# Òr Na Sgliata

# 8  Gold from Slate

September 1689

John accompanied his hosts back to their main
dwellings at the western end of Glencoe. It was a
journey of about a dozen miles, over very rough
terrain, but he hardly noticed that. He was
gripped by the scenery. As they passed through
the eastern entrance to the glen, between the
Great Shepherd and the Devil's Staircase, he
gazed at the high mountains on either side. He
was used to mountains but he'd never seen
anything like these.

"Impressed?" asked Angus, still perched high up
on his plough horse.

"I certainly am. Is it all like this?"

"Aye it is. Our ancestors have lived in between
these mountain walls for hundreds of years and no
one has been able to get in and attack us."

That wasn't strictly true but John accepted it.
They meandered all day through the spectacular
scenery, stopping occasionally for a rest. At one
such place, three rivers met. John could have
watched the movements of the water for hours but
Hector and Donald were keen to get on. They
made another halt, by a little lake called Loch
Achtriochtan, so that Angus' horse and the other
animals could drink. After that there were only a
few short stops, to greet people and swap news. By
evening they were at Donald's croft. John was

56

instantly taken with the flat rocks of the area.

"This is slate!" he said with surprise.

"Is that unusual?" asked Hector.

"I'm a slate quarrier," explained John. "Well, near enough," he told himself.

Hector couldn't see what John was so excited about. Rocks were rocks to him and he got on with the more important work of moving his crippled son back into their home opposite. John would have helped, had he noticed, but he was too engrossed by the stones. When Hector reappeared, he found John breaking bits of rock against each other. The slate was a blue-black colour but what fascinated John was the glistening yellow crystals.

"I've found some gold!" he said, showing a piece to Hector.

"If that is gold, my house is a palace. Every stone has several pieces in it. You Sassenachs* are so simple. Look at this."

He pointed to a cube-shaped hollow in one of the stones of his wall.

"Does gold leave a square hole when it comes out of a rock? Does gold become ... meirgeagh ... in English it is ... Ach."

He shouted some Gaelic through his doorway.

"Rust," came back Angus' voice from within the house.

"You mean these crystals rust?" asked a disappointed John.

"If rust is what water and iron make."

*Sassenach: Englishman, possibly derived from the word, "Saxon".

"Yes, that sounds like rust. Oh. I know what it is. In English we call it Fool's Gold."

Hector looked disdainfully at John. "That is a good name," he observed.

John slept solidly that night, tired from the long trek. He was woken from a dream about gold and slates to be told some breakfast was ready. Angus managed to hobble over from his father's croft* to join the group.

"What do you think of our settlement, John?" he asked.

"I like it. The scenery is beautiful and even the rocks are attractive."

"Yes, my father told me about that. You thought they contained gold."

"In a sense they do."

Angus looked puzzled. "What do you mean?"

"It's like this," explained John. "In England people cut this rock out of the ground. That's my profession," he exaggerated. "The rock splits naturally into flat but strong and weatherproof sheets, which people use to make the roofs on their houses. Unlike the roofs here, which are made of heather, a slate one will last for centuries and it's not just roofs. You can build walls with them too."

Angus was interested. "We use them to make gravestones and small homes. MacIain has some on his roof, in the way you describe, and Castle Stalker to the south of here has such a roof as well. But none of this means there's gold in them. If there was, we

*Croft: Dwelling with a small parcel of land for making a living.

58

would have found an excuse to strip the roof off Castle Stalker years ago."

"There's no need to go that far. You can sell these slates to towns in the Lowlands, maybe even England or Ireland. Think what a difference it would make to this place. It would mean regular work for the men. They could buy food and items for their homes with the money they made. There would be no need to raid other clans for food, animals or household goods. People could build better houses for themselves. There's all sorts of possibilities. I tell you Angus, I have never seen slates as good as these. They must be the best in the world."

Angus was rubbing his beard, exactly as his father did when he was thinking.

"You've given me an idea. My father is very proud of his boat and I love sailing too. We often spend more time at sea than in this glen. Our boat's not big but we could still carry a lot of slates around the coasts. If necessary we could get a bigger one ..."

This was the sort of thing John wanted to hear but Angus stopped, sighed and shook his head.

"Ah, but new ideas are slow to be accepted here. It'll never happen. We'll simply carry on in our traditional ways. So what are you going to do instead, John? Go back to England?"

"Yes, I must. I said I was a slate quarrier. That isn't entirely correct. I'm an apprentice and I have two more years to do before I'm a quarrier in my own right. But after that I could come back here, with the right tools and equipment, in your boat perhaps! Then I could teach you all how to quarry slates and earn some money. I realise that you have your doubts, Angus, but it will have to happen sometime. The world is changing fast and the Highlands must change sooner or later. This way of life can't go on for ever."

"Why not? Folk have lived this way for centuries and are happy with it. The men especially base their reputation, not on digging and labouring but on raiding and warfare." Angus pondered a moment, brooding on his shin before continuing. "I'm not so sure it's worth the cost but that's my problem. Let's talk about your problem instead. How are you going to get home?"

"Your father suggested taking me as far as he could in the boat, the next time you headed my way."

"Yes, he talked to me about that last night." Angus drew John away from the house lest his father should overhear. "The trouble is that he's having second thoughts. He is anxious about the time of year. No one fancies a long sea journey in October. Also, I don't know about your politics and religion, and I won't ask, but you will appreciate that any English Government ships we meet may not look kindly on us. Furthermore, there's hardly a lowland shore where we can stop to rest. You've heard of *Mi-run mor nan Gall?*"

John worked through the words one at a time. "No love great of the Gael?"

"Not bad. It's the Lowlanders' deep hatred of the

60

Highlanders. I don't think you know how dangerous it would be for two Highlanders in a small boat once we sailed beyond the Hebrides."

"Hector didn't make much of these matters before. What changed his mind?"

"I'm not sure. Perhaps it's concern for me, the son he nearly lost. I am all the family he has and he's glad to have me home. He doesn't want to tempt fate again. However, I think we can still help. We could take you some of the way south, as far as the Kintyre peninsular but there we must put about. Even that far is a risk. As for you, it would give you a good start and shorten your journey overland by a great distance. The people also speak English, of sorts."

"How far is Kintyre from the Clyde estuary?"

"It's a few miles the other side. Why do you ask?"

John was thinking of Matthew's cousin, Andrew. "I know of a man in Dumbarton who may be able to help me."

Angus went back to stroking his beard like his father again. "If it's Dumbarton you want, it's on the Clyde, sure enough, but it's not that simple. There are so many inlets and mountains in your way that I believe it would take ten days to walk what a bird could fly in as many minutes. No, the best route is for us to take you to Loch Etive and put you ashore at the Pass of Brander.* From there you could skirt the head of Loch Awe, pass through Glen Array to

*See map of MacIain's later journey on page 109. Much of Angus' description follows it.

61

Inveraray, round the top of Loch Fyne, pass through Glen Kinglas and Glen Croe to Arrochar, follow the shores of Loch Lomond and before long you'll reach Dumbarton."

John was amazed. "Can you read and write?" he asked.

"No. Why?"

"How did you remember all that information? It's as though you had a map in your head. And where did you find such a variety of English words? Your grammar, too, was better than most English people's."

Angus shrugged his shoulders. "I've simply travelled a bit. I spent five years away from here, working on a large ship. I've been to Africa and the Americas. That's how I learned English, from the other swabs on board."

"Remarkable," commented John. "I'll have to write down the directions. How many miles is it?"

Angus didn't give a straight answer. "When we had a matter of honour to settle with certain of clan Campbell, it took us three weeks to do more than that and bring home our reward. It won't take you very long. My father and I need to put to sea soon anyway. We haven't enjoyed fresh sea fish for months and we need some to smoke for the winter. We could take you this week, if you wish."

Angus didn't get a reply and realised why, when he saw John gazing wistfully at Christina.

"Perhaps you don't wish," he mused, and hobbled back to have a word with Hector.

At midday Hector had a word with Donald. In the afternoon, Donald ambled off to the main settlement, at the mouth of the River Coe, and had a word with MacIain. John knew nothing about these conversations but he was at the centre of them.

The first two conspirators, Angus and Hector, were taken with John's business idea and wanted him to stay, or at least come back as soon as possible. They hoped to make a lot of money from transporting slates.

The third conspirator, Donald, had decided to marry Christina off to John. It had only been two months, but in that short time he had watched a definite romance developing between his granddaughter and their guest. Donald himself wasn't romantic so much as practical. He wasn't getting any younger, his son was dead and he needed someone to take care of him in his old age. The easiest way to do that would be to get the best bargain he could for a grandson-in-law. There were plenty of willing suitors, now that Christina's father was out of the way, but John was Donald's preferred choice. No doubt about it, the one with the ideas for making money was the one to encourage.

The fourth conspirator, MacIain, had other problems on his mind. He appeared to the outside world to be a strong and a proud man but, deep down, he was troubled. Highland chieftains measured their importance by the number of armed men they commanded and, in MacIain's case, that number had been seriously reduced. In the three months of the rebellion, not only had he lost more than a fifth of his fighters but he had a corresponding increase in widows and orphans to support. His people were the smallest branch of clan Donald and if he should be called to arms again, or need to raid for food next year, he would be sorely stretched.

John's idea for earning a living, rather than fighting for one, didn't appeal to MacIain's warlord image. He'd prefer to team up with the Appin Stewarts, some other MacDonalds or a group of MacGregors even, to make up his numbers, but other ideas to help him over his problems were worth considering in the meantime. He would have to make further enquiries.

Angus brought an invitation to John that night. "You must be very important. The chief wants you at his house for a dram* or two with him tomorrow."

**Dram:** A measure of whisky.

# 9 The House of MacIain

## Taigh MacIain

# 9 The House of Maclain

September 1689

It was a worried John who set out to meet one of Scotland's most dangerous men. It didn't pay to upset Alasdair MacIain, twelfth chief of the Glencoe MacDonalds. The man held complete control over the area and had an unpleasant tendency to kill anyone who upset him.

"Maybe this wasn't such a good idea after all," thought John but he tried to hide his nerves as he entered the grandest house he'd seen in the Highlands.

John's feet stood on dressed flagstones. Where they weren't overlaid with wooden panelling, the walls too were of dressed stone. There were windows to let the light in and, if necessary, they could be closed with wooden shutters to keep the cold out. That was one reason why it was noticeably warmer here. Another reason was the proper fireplaces, where pine logs burned cheerily and real chimneys carried away the smoke. How different to Donald's croft. There, the heavy smoke from the smouldering peat on the bare earth floor filled the room and choked you, before drifting out of the hole in the roof. MacIain's house even had a flight of stairs up to a second floor, though John wasn't taken up there.

Directly in front of him was a panelled door and John could hear talking and laughter coming from the other side. The talking stopped as he entered. A dozen or so men, mostly with drinks in their hands, turned their attention to him. Then one, the tall man with the mane of long white hair and the handlebar moustache, stepped forward. John recognised a Gaelic greeting and returned what he hoped was a suitable answer, as he gave the man a confident handshake. The handshake belied how John really felt but that, together with his reply, seemed to do the trick. His host smiled and, much to John's relief, continued in English.

"Well sir, what do you think of my house?"

John looked around. Not only was the building grand but the furnishings were some of the best he'd seen anywhere. John was mindful of MacIain's honour and pride as he responded.

"My lord, I have never seen anything as magnificent as this anywhere in the Highlands. It is an honour to be the guest of such a gentleman."

It was a bit over the top to say "lord" and MacIain's enemies would have called him something very different. Nevertheless, it was a good mistake to make, for it did much for the host's dignity. He handed a full cup to John.

"Kind thoughts, young man. A drink to your health and fortune!"

"And to yours, my lord," answered John, before everyone drank deeply. Everyone except John. The twice-distilled spirit was the most powerful drink he'd ever come across and only a little choked him.

The company burst out laughing and one slapped

him heartily on the back. John's eyes watered as he thanked the other guest for his help. Fortunately, they saw his inability to handle their brew as a joke, not an insult. He would have to watch this, for he twigged straightaway what MacIain was up to. The chief intended to loosen John's tongue with alcohol. He would need to keep his wits about him.

John found himself being shown around the room and introduced to the more important folk. There were MacIain's two sons, John and Alasdair, followed by more relatives and some tacksmen. These last men were like little chieftains. They ruled more remote areas but were answerable to MacIain all the same.

"Now, Master Clerk," MacIain concentrated on John. "You've not touched your drink. It's a poor guest that doesn't appreciate his host's spirits. Drink up man!"

"Sir, this must be the strongest drink in the world. Only someone born and bred in Glencoe would be man enough to manage more than a cupful. Forgive this poor Sassenach for drinking it in small amounts."

With that he took a very small one. MacIain seemed impressed with John's argument but disappointed with how little he drank. Still, if the man couldn't handle much, it wouldn't take much to get him talking.

"So, you've met my folk. Tell us about yourself."

John selected his words with care. He began with how he had been found in a church doorway and how he got his name. That caused some laughter and comment, during which time he swapped his nearly full cup with the nearly empty one which the man on his right had put down. Fortunately, apart from MacIain's silver one, the cups were all identical, a set that MacIain had "picked up" on a raid. John went on to talk of how he had become an apprentice quarrier, then took a small sip from his cup to brace himself for what could be a difficult bit. He was reluctant to tell direct lies, so he modified the truth.

"I managed to take some time off from my work in order to see Scotland. I'd heard so much about it. I've found the culture fascinating and the people most hospitable, though none compare with you, my lord."

John paused for the praise to sink in, then he went on.

"However, I believe that I should return home to complete my apprenticeship."

MacIain topped up John's cup, his expression letting slip some surprise at how much he had to pour into it.

"Aye, so I've been told, laddie. I've also been informed that you would like to sell my glen to the English, stone by stone."

This remark caused more laughter and comment, during which John managed to repeat the cup-swapping trick with the man on his left. He was relieved to find that this cup, too, was nearly empty.

"You have a way with words, my lord, and I toast your fine wit!" said John, as he took a gentle swallow.

The others joined in. MacIain stared in disbelief

at the angle of John's cup, though not for long. The men on either side of him both coughed and spluttered uncontrollably. MacIain glared at them.

"It appears that not all Glencoe folk can handle their liquor as well as you suggest, Master Clerk."

He changed the subject back again to John's ideas. John flattered MacIain enough about the value of his slates to persuade him that he could be on to a good thing but MacIain wasn't going to be drawn on the matter.

"I like well what you say but there's a problem. The River Laroch runs down the middle of the slate rocks. That river marks the border between my land and Stewart of Appin's, so half the slates are in my territory and half in his. We would have to come to some kind of arrangement if we were to consider your ideas."

MacIain still hadn't worked out what kind of man he was dealing with so he tested him further with another matter. He had promised Donald he would do so anyway.

"Meanwhile, there's Christina MacColl. There's no hiding the fact young man that she has won your heart and I understand from others that she feels the same about you. I'll come straight to the point. She's a bonnie lassie but she's also an orphan. She needs someone to take care of her and her grandfather. A fine lad like you would make an excellent husband but she needs someone now."

MacIain stared directly into John's eyes. This would prove how genuine the Englishman was.

"If you disappear for two years, she'll have to marry another."

MacIain was bluffing about losing Christina. Thanks to his involvement in the rebellion, MacIain had created a shortage of husbands for all the single women in the glen but John didn't know this and believed what he heard. Nevertheless, he had other things to consider. He swallowed hard before answering as carefully as he could.

"My lord, I confess the girl means more to me than anyone else. I can't imagine the pain of losing her to another man but it is a risk I must take. Let me explain it this way.

"When men hear the name, Alasdair MacIain of Glencoe, what do they feel? Excitement? Respect? Fear perhaps? Your name is more than what men call you. It's a reputation known across the country."

John's comment was quite true. Although numerically one of the least of the Highland clans, the Glencoe MacDonalds were such renowned trouble makers that King William's ministers had even considered using force, to round up the whole clan and dump them in another part of the world. John, though unaware of this, was using the chief's fame to support his argument and continued.

"My lord, I'm equally concerned for my name and reputation. I wrote my signature at the bottom of a legal document and it would cost me my respect if I did not honour what I put my name to."

"And what did this document say?"

"Among other things, I bound myself to my

master for seven years. Also, in that seven years I undertook not to get married. My lord, your people are loyal to you, their master. I must follow their example and be loyal to mine."

Considering John had broken faith with his apprenticeship indenture when he'd joined the army, it was a hollow argument, but nobody there knew what had really happened. John came across as a man of the highest principles. It's funny how nothing destroys the truth more than twisting it very slightly.

MacIain was impressed. He was brilliant at dealing with rogues - after all, he himself was one of the worst - but dealing with an apparently honest man, one who put his principles before his advantage, that was something new. He wasn't sure what to think so concluded indecisively.

"Master Clerk, you have taken an honourable stand in this matter and I respect your wishes. You may leave with Hector and Angus and my blessing goes with you. Meanwhile, I invite you to return in two years' time and we will discuss the situation then. Will you drink to that?"

The issue of Christina was unresolved but the interview could have gone far worse so John agreed.

"I will," he said - and drained his empty cup.

# 10 The Betrothal

# (An Reitich)

# 10 The Betrothal

September 1689

It was long past midnight when John arrived back and his hosts were peacefully asleep. It was very different come the light of day. When John emerged, Christina and Donald were already outside talking to Angus. Christina looked quite angry and, when she faced John, her deep brown eyes burned right through him. He felt uncomfortable.

"John," began Angus, "we've heard some bits of gossip that MacIain offered to let you marry Christina but you turned him down. Is it true?"

"Yes, I suppose I did ... " yawned John. He was about to explain but didn't get a chance, because Angus gave an instant translation. With an angry shout, Christina slapped John across the face and ran off crying. Donald spat contemptuously on the ground and skulked back into his house. Angus reddened and looked up at the mountains.

"Er, I'm not sure how to translate her last sentence," he mumbled.

"No need," winced John. "I felt it in English."

"She has her father's temper but I don't suppose that's why you turned her down. John, I just don't understand you. What happened?"

"Give her some time to calm down, then help me find her. I'll explain everything to you if you can explain it to her."

"What is there to explain?"

"For a start I didn't say I wouldn't marry her."

"But you said..."

"I said one word and you translated before I could finish my sentence. Angus, I do want to marry her. I told MacIain I had to wait."

John went on to explain how he felt it necessary to finish his apprenticeship but, when he had honoured that commitment, he wanted to come back and make Christina his bride.

"In that case I'll help. Mind you, this could be tricky."

Half an hour later, the two of them found Christina sitting by the Laroch stream, casting stones into it. She was still crying and, as each stone went in, she muttered a curse. She pretended not to notice the new arrivals and carried on with her activity, hoping that Angus would translate. He did.

As a stone went in he said, "She wishes that you will remain under the water as long as the stone."

John didn't know quite what to say to that but he wouldn't have had time, anyway. Christina hurried on with her curses. There was another splash.

"May you marry a Campbell. Och! That's a bit mean."

Splash.

"May you never have children."

Splash.

"May your sons die in battle."

"If I don't have any children how can my sons ..."

Splash.

75

"May your breeches rot in Hell."

John couldn't follow the logic of that one either but with the next curse came the answer.

"And when it happens may you still be wearing them," guffawed Angus.

Christina screamed and threw a big rock in, soaking them all.

"That was not funny, you son of a stinking mountain goat."

"I didn't laugh," objected John.

"Didn't you? Oh. Was that one meant for me, then?"

"I don't know and I don't care. Look, this childish behaviour has gone on long enough. Tell her I want to talk to her."

"She says she won't listen."

"Tell her I love her."

"She says you're a liar."

At that point Christina took off again. She was being totally unreasonable and John decided she needed some firm handling. He ran after her and grabbed her by the elbows. She bit and kicked but, no matter how much she struggled, he held her fast.

"She says you're not being fair."

"Neither is she but, if she wants me to let her go, I will - and for good. If she runs away from me once more, it won't just be from me. She'll be running away from my love too and she'll never see me again. The choice is hers."

John gambled his future happiness on that statement - and won. He let go and Christina stopped struggling, though she carried on sobbing. The conversation continued.

"He says again that he loves you, Christina."

"Then why won't he marry me?"

"He wants to."

"Then why did he tell MacIain he wouldn't?"

"He didn't tell MacIain that. He said that he must wait."

Christina calmed down a bit more. "Why?"

"Because he has signed a bit of paper to say he will not marry until he finishes learning his trade."

Christina, who could neither read nor write, and who shared the Glencoe MacDonalds' contempt for legal documents, was not impressed.

"So a piece of paper means more than I do."

"Nothing means more to him than you, but he gave his word before he even knew you existed. Surely you want to marry the sort of man you can trust, whom you can rely on to keep his promises?"

Christina could understand that. "How long must we wait?"

"Two more years. It's a long time and MacIain says you will have to marry someone else before then, in order to support yourself and your grandfather. But John will wait, if you can."

"It's not MacIain's decision or anyone else's. It's mine and I'll wait."

"I don't think you need me any more. I'll leave you two together but, Christina, you don't own John. When a girl gets too possessive about a fellow, he feels trapped and she risks scaring him off and losing him altogether. The secret is to make him think he's chasing you, even when it's the other way round."

On that note, Angus departed, though not before John followed after him a short distance. Outside of Christina's hearing, he asked for one more translation. Then he returned, took Christina's hand and she came voluntarily back to the Laroch. Out came the silk handkerchief again and he gently dried her eyes. When he'd finished, she in turn took the handkerchief, soaked it in the stream and tenderly soothed the red mark across his cheek, the teeth marks in his arms and the scratches on his shins. Then she began removing stones out of the water. She repented over each one and pronounced a blessing in place of each curse, before taking a few more out for luck. John counted them.

"Seventeen?" he asked.

She leaned her head on his breast feeling too guilty to face him.

"More. I couldn't remember them all." She paused.

"Sorry."

"Christina." John sounded solemn. She was apprehensive about what he would say next but she needn't have worried. He asked her what Angus had taught him a few minutes earlier.

*"An Pa's thee nei?"*

For those who can't guess, it was, "Will you marry me?"

*"Posaidh!"* should need no translation.

# 11 Halfway House

## Taigh Leth An Rathad

# 11 Halfway House

September 1689

Christina watched as Hector's boat pulled away from the southern shore of Loch Leven, turned in the lee of Munda's Isle and the pair of sails were hoisted. She gave one last wave of the silk handkerchief when, all too quickly, the boat sped around the headland, carried away by the twelve knot tide at Ballachulish. The lonely figure remained a while on the shoreline, waiting for the tears to clear, before returning to the settlement.

Meanwhile, John sat fingering a lock of thick jet-black hair in his hand. He was still doing so two days later, as he was put ashore. He thanked Hector and Angus and asked them to pass on his love to Christina, before heading along the route they pointed out. How he wished for their company. Despite Angus' optimism, and John's meticulous notes, it took him ten days to reach Dumbarton. The few folk he met on the way, some of whom spoke a little English, had been exceptionally hospitable but he'd spent most of the October nights with very little shelter, and only the small plaid wrapped around him for warmth.

So it was that he found himself, hungry and looking the worse for wear, standing outside the thick panelled door of Andrew Smith's house. Despite the time he'd had to think it over, he still wasn't sure what to say. Before knocking, he decided to seek some extra help. If the John of a year earlier could have seen what happened next, he would not have believed it. There he was, leaning against the door, praying. He got a few odd looks from the passers-by but he wasn't aware of them.

"Dear God, you've brought me through so much. I survived the rout at Killiecrankie and avoided drowning on Rannoch Moor. I've been fed and sheltered by the enemy. Only you could have arranged that. Now I'm back in civilization. I need to say thank you but I still need to ask you for more help. Please keep Christina for me, and, right now, let me be accepted back by all those folk I've known before. I don't consider you very often, it's true, but I have come here on my way to make amends, haven't I? I am doing what's right, aren't I? Please give me credit for that."

No sooner had he finished, than the door opened unexpectedly and John fell backwards, into the hall and onto the floor.

"I wondered what folk were staring at on my doorstep," came the harsh voice of Andrew's house maid. "A drunken vagabond. Be off with you before I get the menservants and the dogs," she scolded, enforcing her feelings with a broom.

"Please, Janet. Do you not recognize me?"

The combination of her name and an English accent temporarily took the wind out of her sails and, as she paused, John took the opportunity to get to his feet and address her. He remembered how poorly she presented herself, her large bitter face made worse by uncut matted hair tied with string.

"It's me, John Clerk. I came here with Matthew Smith, you know, Mr. Smith's cousin. It was some months back. Is your master at home?"

Janet remembered who John was and the memory seemed to reawaken the dragon in her.

"Aye, he is but why should he be wanting to have dealings with such a one as you, you who rejected his hospitality the first time and reneged on his cousin to boot?"

She raised her broomstick again but fortunately John was saved as Andrew peered round a door.

"Is that any way to welcome a visitor, Janet? I warrant that one day I'll catch you flying on that broomstick of yours."

Janet lowered her weapon and John heaved a sigh of relief. Andrew disappeared into his parlour.

"I thought I recognized your voice, sir," he called back. "Come in here, if you please. Janet, I'll take supper in here tonight and Master Clerk shall dine with me."

Thankfully, John edged his way round the broomstick and, although it followed him closely, it didn't hurt him again. There again, John wasn't certain that Janet's scowl wasn't more painful. Politely he knocked on the open door.

"Come in," responded Andrew solemnly, "and shut the door after you."

Andrew sat at a table with a heavy volume in front of him. John guessed which book it was and suspected that he was going to get a lecture from it but, mercifully, it didn't materialize. Andrew simply rested his chin on his clasped hands, stared over his spectacles at John and said nothing. Had he not mentioned dining, John would have found the silence even more uncomfortable. Then Andrew's manner seemed to change and there was almost the hint of a smile as he raised his eyebrows.

"And what were you doing on my doorstep?" he enquired.

"Praying, sir."

Andrew's eyebrows dropped as he warned John not to act up to him.

"It's true, sir."

"If so, what were you praying, may I ask?"

"That I'd be let in."

Andrew's eyes regained their twinkle. "Well, well. I doubt Janet realised that she was an answered prayer when she landed you on the floor. What else did you pray?"

"Thanks that I'd survived the rout at Killiecrankie and avoided drowning on Rannoch Moor and that God would preserve and keep Christina for me."

Andrew closed his eyes and put his hand to his forehead. "Dear me," he said. "This will take some unravelling. Killiekrankie, Rannoch Moor, drowning. And ..." there was a glint in his eye, " ... who might Christina be? It seems you have a lot of explaining to do."

He placed his spectacles on the Bible and moved it to one side to make room for Janet as she knocked and entered to lay the table. She smiled with deference at Andrew but scowled at John at every opportunity. Inevitably, before the meal commenced, Andrew said a long prayer of thanks, which included a lot about John. John felt ravenous and was glad when the long grace came to an end but he had little time to tuck in heartily, for Andrew wished to hear more.

"Now, young man, some time ago, you disappeared from this house and tonight you have reappeared. I should be interested to hear a full explanation of what happened in between. I fancy a fine story but I must warn you that I want a truthful one. Understood?"

John nodded. "Certainly, but ..." he hesitated, "... but may I have your word that all this will be kept confidential?"

Andrew assented. "You have it. Now, perhaps we could start from the very beginning?"

By the time the meal had ended, John had given Andrew a frank account, pausing only when Janet was present with her duties.

"Well, my young adventurer, that's quite an escapade. I'll need to muse longer on what you've told me but it's getting late. I'll ask Janet to make you up a bed for the night and we'll discourse further in the morning. Before that, could you pass me back my Bible? There's a page I was reading earlier which seems relevant to today and I'd like to meditate further on what I've been reading."

With that he instructed Janet accordingly and

bade John good-night. John slept solidly for the first time in weeks, thanks to a comfortable bed. He awoke late and came down to find Andrew had had breakfast and was busy penning a letter. John ate in the kitchen, under Janet's scowling gaze, and was relieved when Andrew sent for him.

"Have you heard of the prodigal son?" Andrew enquired.

"Yes, I have. It's a story Jesus told about a young man who walked out on his father and got himself into a lot of trouble. He realised what a fool he'd been and went back to his home, to say sorry and seek his father's help. His father welcomed him back, though he didn't deserve it. I noticed that you had your Bible open at that page last night."

"You're an observant young man and I think you can see similarities to your own situation. I've written this letter to my cousin Matthew and asked him if he will do the same for you as the father in the story did for his son. What I haven't written, but I'll say to you, is that if he won't accept you back there's a place for you here." Andrew gave John an encouraging smile. "But let's hope that won't be necessary, eh?"

"Thank you, sir."

"Very well, I want you to be ready to leave tomorrow morning and take this letter with you. I will arrange and pay for your transport to Carlisle. You'll have to make your own way from there. Have you anything to say?"

"Only thank you, again. Thank you very much."

Then John thought of something else. "There's just one puzzle. What have I done to upset Janet?"

Andrew shook his head. "You're simply a handsome youth ..."

"Is that a crime?" John interjected.

" ... and I might add an impatient one. I was going to say - before you interrupted - that you appear similar, in age and looks, to another one she knew many years ago, in Perth."

"Perth? So she's of Highland origin?"

"That's so, though the lad concerned came from Edinburgh. He made her to feel she was special to him and she fell hopelessly in love. I'm sure it was genuine on her part but to him it was just a passing infatuation. She asked him to marry her, when she found herself expecting their child, but he deserted her at the first opportunity. She was cast out of her home and came to Edinburgh, seeking the father of her bairn. It's a long story but, not only could she not trace the father, she also lost the child. She's hated young men ever since, even though she's old enough to be a grandmother these days. It's so sad. Years later and she still cannot forgive, still makes herself unattractive. Er ... John, pardon me for asking but, this Christina, she's not likely to find herself ..."

"I didn't even kiss her," insisted John, "and I'll return."

"Hmm," thought Andrew. "I'm glad to hear the first bit but that second statement ... I can foresee trouble ahead."

# 12 Absence Makes the Heart Grow Fonder

*Mor as motha an astar
san as mor a tha gradh*

## 12  Absence Makes the Heart Grow Fonder

October 29th 1689

John approached Matthew and Hannah's door and knocked but the response was not encouraging. The occupants were in no mood to open the door after nightfall.

"Who is it and what do you want?" Matthew demanded.

John was put out by the severity of the reply.

"It's John Clerk, sir. I ... I ... I've come back."

John was prepared to be sent away with a flea in his ear but quite the reverse happened. The bolts were thrown back and Matthew flung open the door.

"John! It really is you. Hannah! Come quickly. John's back!"

Hannah rushed to the door and flung her arms around John. She couldn't believe it. John was whisked inside and sat down at a table and, while Matthew read his cousin's letter, Hannah laid out a large supper. In between mouthfuls, John told his story. Hannah, especially, was quite shocked by some of it. As the eating and storytelling came to an end John decided to get the important matter sorted out.

"Matthew," he began, "when you read the Bible to me, you read a story about a young man who left his home and made a complete fool of himself."

Matthew nodded. "The prodigal son. I've just read a reminder about him," he said, tapping his cousin's opened letter.

"That's him," John confirmed. "Well, I know now how he felt. It took me just a few months to make a wreck of my life. It began when I abused your trust and ran away from my apprenticeship. There's no excuse. I was wrong and I want to say I'm sorry. You used to speak of forgiveness." Then, thinking of Janet, he went on, "Can you forgive me?"

Matthew's face was sad yet his voice was kind. "I welcome your apology. I accept it and, yes, of course I forgive you. I would be a hypocrite if I spoke about forgiveness and didn't demonstrate it, wouldn't I?"

He got up from his chair opposite John, walked over to an old chest and drew out a piece of parchment with a wavy edge at the bottom.

"You recognise this?" he asked.

"Of course I do. It's my apprenticeship indenture. The copy with the corresponding indentations used to live in my old room."

"Not necessarily your old room, John. It still is your room and the indenture is still there. It's still valid, too, if you want to take it up again."

John was delighted. "I certainly would." Then his smile dropped. "Is it that easy? After all the hurt I've caused you?"

"No. It's not easy. For many months, Hannah has wept much and we've both prayed for you daily. We wanted you back as though you were the son we never had. Sometimes we doubted whether you were alive and, indeed, from what we've heard you shouldn't be but God clearly heard our prayers. The relief is indescribable. You say you know how the prodigal son felt. I'm beginning to understand how the father felt! I'm in the mood to forgive and forget and put the past behind us."

Matthew's hand was held out. John took it and gave it the sort of squeeze which says things that words can't.

Matthew responded by saying, "Very well. That's settled. Now off to your bed. You must be back at the quarry face in the morning, at five o'clock."

So it was that John set to work for another two years, to fulfil his obligations to Matthew. Little of importance happened in that time. Suffice to say John endured two very lonely years. He couldn't keep Christina out of his mind. Would she really wait for him? Would he return to Glencoe and find her married to someone else? Was she still alive even? The hard part was simply not knowing. Not knowing had become unbearable, come the December that John completed his interrupted apprenticeship. Even though Matthew offered him a job in the same quarry, he turned it down. He wanted to get back to the Highlands immediately.

As John packed to leave, possibly for the last time, Matthew had a heart-to-heart talk with him. He knew about his ideas for Glencoe. He wasn't entirely against them but he questioned whether John was mature enough at 22 to take on such a great enterprise. It wasn't just the work. There were problems of language and culture and, with all the recent troubles, the Western Highlands were no safe place for an Englishman to live. Then there were other questions.

What if MacIain should demand that John take up arms for him against the rightful monarchs or to raid and steal? John said that he would make it a condition of his service that he was not to be involved in such matters.

"Easier said than done," thought Matthew but he knew deep down that he couldn't persuade John otherwise while Christina was on his mind.

"You realise how few couples betrothed so young have successful marriages."

"True, but my age no longer ends with "teen" and soon Christina's won't either."

Matthew changed tack.

"Sharing all your thoughts and ideas with your spouse is vital if your marriage is to survive. You haven't even explained to your wife-to-be that you'd fought on the other side at the battle where her father was killed, have you? It would be hard enough if you spoke the same language, but you don't. She knows none of yours and what little you know of hers is rusty now."

"When I was born, Matthew, I couldn't speak any language. I learned English easily enough. Gaelic will be the same. Anyway, it's the language of the Garden of Eden. That should make you happy."

"Who spun you that yarn, John?"

"Angus did. He said that, many years ago, a

Scottish king put two new born babies on an island, with only a dumb nurse to look after them. After a few years they were taken off the island and presented to the king. They spoke to him in pure Gaelic, so it must be the language of Eden."

"I know that story too. Did Angus tell you the end of it? Gaelic was also the language of the ferryman who took the supplies to the island but nobody had the courage to tell the king that. Neither, it appears, did your friend, Angus, have the honesty to tell you.

"That apart, there are more important matters than her language. What of the girl's religious beliefs?"

John could tell that Matthew was about to preach and braced himself.

"From what you've told me, her spiritual values amount to little more than a few odds and ends of Roman Catholicism, mixed with a mountain of superstition. On top of that, she takes advice from a witch and puts curses on people. Who knows what attitudes she may have picked up from her father, a violent drunkard? Be sure of this, if you marry a child of the Devil, you can expect problems with your father-in-law."

John rarely got angry with Matthew but that last remark went too far. He grabbed the older man by the lapels and banged him against the wall.

"Nobody talks about my wife-to-be like that, not even you, Matthew Smith."

Even as he did it, John regretted his action.

"I'm sorry, Matthew," he said as he let go and

began to straighten the ruffled lapels. "I shouldn't have done that ... but ... but surely you must remember what it's like to fall in love?"

Matthew recovered his composure.

"Of course I do. It happened to me yesterday."

"What? You? Who with?"

"My wife."

"Matthew. Don't be childish."

"It's not childish. It's true. Thirty years on and I still worship her, which is why I can understand your reaction just now. I'm sorry for the way I phrased things but I must say that had you insulted Hannah, I wouldn't have seized your lapels and pushed you against a wall."

"No, you wouldn't have," admitted an ashamed John.

"No, I'd have thrown you clean through it and out the other side!"

John gave Matthew a big grin.

"Thanks, Matthew. You're a good man. I couldn't have had a better master. You and Hannah have brought me so far in life. You've both done me proud and I'm grateful. Nevertheless, I've got to work things out for myself from now on. I'm sure you understand that."

Matthew did. He had the sense to realise that he couldn't hold on to John. Though childless, he understood what it felt like to say goodbye to a son, possibly forever. It was an even worse wrench for Hannah.

"Couldn't you wait for Christmas, John?" she

pleaded. "Even if you must marry this girl, why not bring her back here? I could make up for the mother she never knew, be a grandmother to your children perhaps ..."

Hannah was getting weepy and John couldn't cope. He gently changed the subject before taking his leave of them. It was a ridiculous time to travel but John's craving to see Christina and find out what had happened in the last two years got the better of him. He set off with just a pony, a change of clothes, some coins, food and a few tools on another pony. Matthew asked John to take a letter to his cousin, Andrew, in Dumbarton. John didn't know what it was about but the message behind the wax seal was to do with him. It asked Andrew to give John some food and shelter, try and persuade him to give up his foolish journey but, if unsuccessful, to provision him for the rest of it.

Everyone thought the lonely figure on his pony was stupid as he departed through the wintry weather. Stupid he was, but not alone. Matthew and Hannah's prayers, together with the One who heard them, saw to that.

# 13  Friends on the Journey

# Cairdean Air Turas

# 13   Friends on the Journey

December 31st 1691

Most folk's Hogmanay* celebrations were getting underway when a cold, tired and hungry John reached the ferry at Loch Creran. He gazed in frustration at the aggravating sea inlet between himself and the opposite bank. He was now only a few miles south of Glencoe but he would have to walk as many miles again to get round this obstacle. Still, he wouldn't have made it this far had it not been for Andrew in Dumbarton. Andrew's house was still a welcoming place and even more so since Janet had changed for the better. John could hardly believe the difference. She'd clearly had some kind of religious experience and kept using words like, "Forgiven" and "New Creation." John didn't care for the spiritual stuff but he was glad that she treated him so much better, especially as she reserved her broom solely for sweeping these days. Andrew brought John up to date with what had been happening in Scotland during the two years he'd been away.

"I'm glad to say, John, that despite the fears of another uprising to replace William with James, we've seen very little trouble here. There's been the odd incident in the Highlands but most chiefs

*Hogmanay: Name for New Year celebrations in Scotland, where much more is made of the event than in England.

have remained at home, still licking their wounds from the rebellion in 1689. Last year, even MacIain and the other MacDonalds did nothing to stop the new Fort William being built in their part of the world and being garrisoned with redcoats.

"I'm glad we don't live in Ireland, though. It's been a different story over there. James looked like capturing and controlling the whole country until William defeated him at the Battle of the Boyne. Let's hope it's the end of the Irish troubles.

"Now the Highlands are the last Jacobite stronghold and, even here, there's likely to be a peaceful settlement. King William is considering buying off the chiefs. As part of the bargain, he has promised a free pardon to all the clans who fought against him at Killiecrankie, provided their chiefs take an oath of allegiance to him by the end of this year."

John thought of MacIain and the other chiefs. He couldn't see them swapping kings too easily.

"How did the chiefs take the offer?"

"From what I heard, they had mixed feelings. They sent messengers to James, now a refugee in France, to see if he would allow them to switch their loyalty. They had to know as soon as possible because of the deadline which William set. He threatened them that any who didn't take the oath before the New Year would face dire consequences, though he didn't say what. I'm afraid I don't know any more but, John, listen to me. This is a very precarious time to be going to Glencoe. You're more

97

than welcome to stay here or let me help you go back to my cousin. Either way, I strongly advise you to keep away from the Highlands, at least until January, when we may know what MacIain has done about this oath."

Andrew's warning was more serious than either of them realised but John was keen to get moving again. Andrew couldn't talk him out of the journey but, having similar beliefs to his cousin, he insisted on praying with John before he left. John felt less resentful than he once would have done and thanked the old man for his kindness. He thanked him even more as his host put some silver coins in his hand and closed his fingers round them. John had no idea how expensive his journey would be and those coins made all the difference.

Now, he was at the ferry, all his food was gone and he was penniless again. The ferryman, noting John's uncommon dress, asked in English if he wanted to be rowed over the narrow inlet. John thanked him for the offer but said he would ride the ten miles or so round the creek. The man was used to this talk and thought John wanted to bargain for the fare but, once he found out that there was genuinely no money, he happily gave up. It was bitterly cold and he could go back to his celebrations instead. He even felt sorry for John and invited him in for some food and drink. Once again John was grateful for some Scottish hospitality.

"Aye, you're welcome for a break here, young man. Where are you going?"

"Clencloe," slurped John, over his cup of warm broth.

The man looked interested. "Pardon me. It's not my concern, I know, but can you tell me why you are headed there?"

"Happily. I'm going to claim my bride."

The man shrugged his shoulders and took a bite to eat. He carried on speaking with his mouth full.

"Congratulations. I didn't wish to pry. It's just that I thought you might be able to enlighten me. I ferried MacIain and his gillies to this side of the water only a couple of hours ago."

"That's strange," replied John. "I didn't pass them on the road."

"It is so. As they landed they were captured at gun point by redcoats. They are prisoners in the dungeons of that castle over there."

John was about to ask for more information but they were interrupted by the arrival of another man needing the ferry. He was well dressed, in his thirties and mounted on a fine horse.

"Alan!" exclaimed the ferryman. "What are you doing about in this cold weather? I expected you to be snug at home enjoying Hogmanay."

"I'm afraid I must be about my business, whatever the season, James. However, if you get myself and my horse across now, I shall be home just as things get lively. But excuse me. You won't get three horses in the boat. Was this gentleman ahead of me?"

"That's all right. He's a Sassenach who prefers to

ride around the loch. No doubt, you will want to practise your English on him."

Alan would. He was by nature a show off but, more crucial, Alan was one of King James' undercover agents and John's unlikely presence concerned him. What was an Englishman doing here at such a time? Was he really a poor man, taking the longer route because he hadn't the fare, or was he up to something else? Maybe a gesture of help would reveal more. The trouble was, he didn't want to insult the fellow by offering to pay his fare. No matter, there was a way round that problem.

"I understand you are a visitor to these parts," he began. "Are you heading north?"

"I am, sir, to Glencoe."

"Well, these are wild paths we ride. They are not always safe. To be honest," he lied, "I would be glad of some company. If I can meet your expenses across the loch, would you do me that honour?"

John certainly would. With suitable words of appreciation he accepted. A reluctant ferryman set off through the snowy weather to get his boat ready. As they waited, John's new companion set up a conversation. Why was an Englishman visiting such an obscure place as Glencoe at that time of year? John told him he had friends by the River Laroch whom he had promised to visit.

"Ah, Laroch. I know a few folk there myself. Might your friends be the same as mine?"

"Perhaps. There's Hector MacDonald and his son, Angus. Have you met them?"

"Hector with the boat? Aye, I ken* the family well. Angus accompanied me once, when I visited acquaintances to the north. The weather was too bad to use the boat so we went by horse. Do you know, he used a massive great plough horse. I don't know where he got it from but it wasn't very practical. I had many folk to see but I do believe Angus rode the slowest old plodder in the Highlands."

John could just imagine it. He remembered why Angus first rode the creature.

"How is Angus' leg?" he enquired. "He'd, em, he'd had a mishap when I last saw him, a couple of years back."

"Och, he still has a limp but it doesn't worry him. He's as cheerful as can be these days. He wed a year ago, to a remarkable young lady. They say she was very good looking once upon a time. Sadly, she was gored by a bull shortly before the wedding. She was left a cripple and her fine face suffered terribly. Nevertheless, Angus must have loved her for her personality and not for her looks. He went ahead and married her all the same and right happy they both are now. When he and I returned from our travels, she had produced a fine young daughter for him, a bonnie wee lassie. She has her mother's thick hair and deep brown eyes. She'll break many a young man's heart when she's older. Will you be seeing Alasdair MacIain by any chance?"

"I expected to but the ferryman said that some

*Ken: to know a person, as opposed to knowing information.

101

soldiers had arrested him on his way south, at this very spot only a few hours ago. He and his men are being held captive in a local castle."

Alan grabbed John's shoulder. His casual manner had slipped.

"What did you say?"

John repeated it.

Alan lapsed into his native language as he talked to himself. Then he started on the ferryman, who had just returned. The pair of them carried on an animated conversation until Alan remembered John.

"Oh, forgive me, friend. I forgot some business. I regret I can't join you on the ferry after all but I'll keep to my offer. You'd better cross now while the tide and weather are reasonable."

As John sat in the boat, he would have wondered much at what was going on if Alan's parting remark hadn't hit him so hard.

"Have a good journey to Laroch. When you see them, give Alan Stewart's best wishes to Angus, Christina and the wee bairn."

## Oidhche Challainn

# 14 Unusual Hogmanay

December 31st 1691

John continued the last few miles feeling numb, and not from cold. How could they do this to him? Angus was supposed to be a friend. Christina had promised to wait for him. The numbness turned to anger, as two years of frustration boiled over, and, by the time John reached Ballachulish, he was pushing his ponies to their limits. He was going to go straight to Angus and Christina and let them know what he thought of them and the way they had betrayed his trust. He had a few choice words and phrases lined up when he arrived at Hector's croft.

John banged loudly on the door and, when Hector proved slow in answering, he banged again, much louder this time. Hector finally opened the door and stared in surprise.

"John! I didn't expect to see you here."

"I'm sure you didn't. Where can I find Angus and Christina?"

"In Donald MacColl's old home opposite. They moved in when he died."

"Right! I'll go and see them straightaway!"

With that he strode purposefully through the snow to the house where he'd once been a guest. The door shook as he struck it. He got a command in Gaelic and, although he hadn't heard the language for two years, he got the idea it was something about quiet and a baby waking. He'd wake the baby alright. He was enraged enough to wake the whole glen. The door opened and a lady with a mauled, now almost repulsive, face berated him. She clearly didn't recognise him and stepped to one side as Angus appeared to deal with the intruder.

"John! I didn't expect to see you here."

"That's exactly what your father said," replied John, though a tinge of doubt was appearing in his voice. "Who is this?" he asked.

"This magnificent lady is Christina Rankin, my wife. Come in John. I've lots to tell you. You must be cold, man, and Hogmanay is no time to be outside. Christina has prepared some fine food for later but you're welcome to some now. Christina MacColl is a fine cook, I'll grant you, but nobody can satisfy a man's appetite like my Christina can."

John felt a fool but also relieved. He'd forgotten how common a name Christina was around here. This one also had thick ginger hair, not black. His pulse quickened.

"Thank you for your invitation but I'd like to meet my own Christina first. Where is she?"

"She moved in with Catherine MacDonald after they laid her father to rest on Munda's Isle. She's helping at the house of one of MacIain's sons. They've just had a daughter and the mother's poorly. However, I expect she'll be home soon."

"Excuse me," said John, getting up and heading for the door. "I'm sure you'll understand."

"Of course," smiled Angus. "We'll see you later."

John bolted down the track which ran beside the loch. Within a few minutes he saw a figure coming the other way. She stopped as she saw him approaching. Despite being short of breath John managed to call her name. She recognised his voice and ran, as fast as her long skirt allowed, to meet him. They flung their arms around each other and John swung Christina off the ground and round and round a couple of times. When he stopped they were both laughing. Then they simply grinned at each other.

Both had changed in those two years. John's beard was less wispy and his shoulders broader. He'd matured more as a person but little else showed. Christina, on the other hand had blossomed. She had progressed from a pretty teenager, whose looks were still childlike sometimes, to a beautiful woman. Her facial features were more definite and she had grown slightly taller. John took the lock of hair, which she had given him earlier, and held it up to the much longer hair which flowed over her brightly coloured shawl and some way down her back. It had become even thicker in that two years.

As the light faded, they walked back to Laroch, hand in hand. The conversation was limited but they were happy. John determined to get back to learning the language as soon as he could.

As they approached the little collection of crofts they found Catherine was also watching out for Christina. She scolded them both for the shameful way they held hands in public. Secretly though, she was pleased.

Although it was a squash, the evening was spent in merriment with other folk in Angus and Christina's croft. Hector offered John a home with himself until the wedding. In the meantime, they would all help to build John and Christina a home of their own.

John was so happy that he forgot to mention what he'd heard of MacIain's fate. That was probably a good thing, for it would have spoiled the festivities if he had. Little did the happy folk know it, but their chief was only half way through a difficult week.

His problems began long before his arrest, and in France rather than Scotland. Despite the deadline for the oath of allegiance, James sat around in Paris and dithered for several months. It wasn't until December that he finally gave permission for the chieftains to swear their loyalty to William.

On the 12th of December, with the deadline only nineteen days away, a messenger left Paris to take the news to the Scottish Highlands. He arrived in London about the 17th. Remarkably, he managed to continue on horseback through the wintry weather to reach Edinburgh by the 21st. Understandably, he could go no further. Fresh messengers tried to meet the deadline but the arctic conditions made it an impossible task to get the news through the mountains.

Alan had been one of these envoys and he had managed to get the message to MacIain in Glencoe that he was free to take the oath of allegiance to King William. Then, as he told John, he had gone north, with Angus as a guide. This was to inform other small and remote clans of the news.

Whilst Alan and Angus were on their mission, Alasdair MacIain went to perform his oath to Colonel John Hill at Fort William. He was just in time, he believed, but in reality he had made a disastrous mistake. Colonel Hill had no authority to accept the oath. It had to be performed before a sheriff at Inveraray, far to the south and deep in Campbell country.

This information struck fear into MacIain and his gillies. The Campbells hated him, and with just cause. Much of his wealth had been theirs before he had stolen it off them. Now he was required to pass through their territory and submit to one of their judges. Worse still, MacIain had been in front of the justices at Inveraray before, awaiting execution for murder and his captors' delight at finally nailing him had turned to fury when he had escaped. His return would be too good an opportunity for his enemies, who included almost everyone in Inveraray, too miss. Allistair MacIain cleared his throat as he realised he was fingering his neck.

Sensing the problem, John Hill wrote the worried man a covering letter, addressed personally to the sheriff. Armed with this, the anxious chieftain braved the snow and the risks and set off back the way he had come. He crossed the ferry at Ballachulish, bypassed his home and followed the

N
W   E
S

Fort William

Ben Nevis

Glen Nevis

Kinlochleven

Ballachulish
Ferry →

Rannoch
Moor

Glencoe

Loch Linnhe

Castle
Stalker

Maclain
arrested
here

Maclain's
route to
Inverary
from Fort
William.

Loch Creran

Loch Etive

Barcaldine
Castle

(Maclain
imprisoned
here for
24 hours)

Ferry

Pass of
Brander

Loch Awe

Glen Orchy

Scale:
1inch
=5miles

Glen Array

Glen Fyne

Inverary

Loch Fyne

Glen
Kinglass

Glen
Croe

Loch Lomond

coast to Creran. As he disembarked from the ferry, he had the misfortune to be spotted by redcoats. They were highly suspicious about what this notorious renegade was up to and pulled him in for questioning. This was the incident which the ferryman reported to John. MacIain pleaded that he had a letter from Colonel Hill and must be at Inveraray in only a matter of hours but it fell on deaf ears. Once he was eventually released, his deadline had well and truly passed.

The exhausted little party not only arrived too late in Inveraray but they found that the Sheriff was away. On his return, he refused to accept any vows from this latecomer. There were no excuses and it was only when the broken old man fell on his knees and cried like a child that Sir Colin Campbell relented. He administered the oath but gave no guarantee that it would be accepted.

MacIain and his small party returned home. Everyone in the glen believed they were now safe under their new king's protection but they were wrong. The list of those who had taken the oath was sent to Edinburgh. A clerk checking the documents noticed that the Glencoe MacDonalds' chief had submitted six days late and, after some discussion, a seventeenth-century bureaucrat put a line through Alasdair MacIain's name.

He passed on the documents with ink on his fingers - and blood on his hands.

# 15 Unlikely Guests

## Cairdean Neo-Choltach

# 15 Unlikely Guests

February 1st 1692

John glanced behind to make sure Catherine wasn't watching them. Finding it was all clear, he put his arm around Christina's shoulder, as the pair of them surveyed the beginnings of their new home. It wasn't much to look at yet. The stones were only now peeking out above ground level.

One reason why it was taking so long was because the house was much larger than its neighbours. John planned to have more than one room. From the entrance, there would be a combined living room and kitchen, with a proper fire for cooking and a chimney to take the smoke away. The floor would be of slate, not earth, and as they walked over it, suitably placed rugs would keep their feet warm. Beyond that room would be a bedroom. John remembered how, on his first vissit, they shared one room for everything and the only privacy Christina had was to sleep behind her loom. Joined to the house, but with a separate entrance, would be a byre for the animals. John refused to share his living accommodation with sheep, cows and chickens, the way he'd done till now. His tools could live there as well. Their home would be second only to MacIain's.

He even planned on a floor above his bedroom. This would act as a ceiling for him, and a bedroom under the eaves for his children. The family and any guests would be protected from the elements by a slate roof.

The neighbours considered this too ambitious and even Christina thought so at first, until John told her that nothing but the best would do for her. The best was taking a lot longer and another thing was hindering the work. January in the Highlands was not an ideal time for working outside. Daily, John had to clear the snow away from where he laboured. Even with the heavy toil, it was hard to keep warm. With such weather, the neighbours preferred to stay indoors as much as possible and became less enthusiastic about their earlier offers of help.

Never mind, John reassured Christina in his halting Gaelic. It would go faster in the spring.

John and Christina turned from the foundations of their new house to admire the view intended to greet them from their doorway. They were distracted by activity at the Ballachulish ferry. A boat was crossing to their side with some red figures in it. John recognised straight away what they were and called the neighbours over. He pointed out what was going on, as another boatload of soldiers crossed the narrow waters.

"It's alright," commented one. "It's just a small patrol heading south, along by the coast."

"I'm not so sure," answered another. "A second boatload is on its way across while the first group has formed up and is heading this way. What could they want with us?"

No one wanted to wait and find out. A young

runner was dispatched with a warning to Glencoe village, a mile away, while everyone else grabbed their valuables and followed.

As the troops approached the village they found their way blocked by the chief's eldest son, John MacIain, together with some well-armed supporters. The Laroch folk had taken refuge behind them. There was a command to halt and John listened as a parley took place.

The soldiers had no ill intentions, they said. There was a shortage of space at Fort William and they had official papers requesting the locals to billet the men temporarily. The people of Glencoe were asked to do this to make up for the taxes they hadn't paid. The MacDonalds, who had avoided all taxes in living memory, couldn't argue about that but they were still highly suspicious. Not only were there around two hundred soldiers, they were also men of Campbell of Argyll's regiment. It seemed more natural to face them across a battlefield than a dinner table.

Not everyone was happy but MacIain accepted the officers' words and papers as genuine. He ordered his people to provide hospitality for the newcomers. So many of them were there, that they had to be spread over several miles, all the way from the Laroch to far up Glencoe.

Catherine and Christina had very little room but they were ordered to accept two soldiers. Catherine was in a state of panic so John pretended that he lived with them and there was only room for one more. Catherine was shocked at the way John wormed his way into living with his fiancée. John pointed out that he had shared a house with her before. That was before they'd got engaged, she retorted. Now it was different. John couldn't follow Catherine's logic but he reckoned John and one soldier under the roof was better than no John and two soldiers. Hector got landed with the other one. He would have preferred to have kept John but he understood the problem.

The soldier allocated to Catherine's house was only eighteen. John admired his smart uniform and excellent equipment. He'd have taken more pride in his occupation if he had been so well equipped as a soldier. Then his envy grew to jealousy when he saw Christina admiring the lad too. John hastily moved to put a stop to it.

"This is my fiancée, Christina MacColl," he interrupted. "My name is John Clerk and this is Catherine MacDonald." He used English for the benefit of the soldier.

Catherine couldn't understand all that John said but the gist of it made her cross. First John had moved uninvited into her home and now he rubbed salt into the wound by doing the introductions. This was her house and therefore the honours should have been hers. She took over the conversation and invited their visitor to introduce himself. His name was James MacDiarmid and, despite his uniform, he was more fluent in Gaelic than English. This disconcerted John. This interloper would soon be chatting up Christina better than he could. Feeling unwelcome, John decided to talk to Angus instead. He was always good company. He found him heading away with the plough horse.

"Where are you taking that?"

"As far away as I can. Did you hear the name of the captain in charge of those soldiers? It was Robert Campbell of Glenlyon!"

"So what's the problem? Does he eat horses?"

"Idiot! Don't you remember when we first met? Where did I tell you I got this beast from?"

"You said it was a place called Glenly ... Oh, I see. Could be embarrassing."

"You'd better get back and help the others hide things. There's not a croft in Glencoe hasn't got something of his. Our visit bankrupted him. Keep an especial eye on that soldier you've been landed with."

No-one in Catherine's house need have worried. They had acquired nothing which concerned James MacDiarmid and he turned out to be a very likeable lad. Catherine was impressed, especially since MacDiarmids belonged to clan Campbell. John too soon found he was no rival. James actually admired John's building work and even found time to carry slates for him. There was just one job he didn't help with.

Whenever it had been too cold outside, John had occupied himself with another sort of present for Christina. A week after James arrival it was finished, a proper gravestone for Christina's

116

grandfather and John's former host, Donald MacColl.

The epitaph also gave Christina's parents a mention. Not content with an inscription, John added a beautiful engraving of a thistle. In a way, it reminded him of Christina, a prickly character but beautiful.

That afternoon, when James' military duties were over, he came to help John ferry the stone to Donald's grave on the island. As they struggled to load it into Hector's boat, a man on horseback approached them.

"Alan! I last saw you at the Loch Creran ferry. What are you doing here?"

As usual, Alan wasn't going to let on.

"Just passing by on the way home," he pretended. "I came over to see what you were doing."

"James and I were just off to erect a gravestone for Christina's grandfather. I made it myself."

"Did you now? Well, it's a fine piece of craftsmanship, though it looks heavy. I'd be pleased to give you a hand. Have you room for one more?"

Alan's offer had less to do with helping John than taking the opportunity to extract information from an individual soldier with an unguarded tongue. The truth was that Alan's clan, the Appin Stewarts, hadn't sworn the oath and were nervous about the large number of soldiers right on the very edge of their territory. He opened the conversation casually.

"Are you going to shoot a rabbit or two for the pot when we get to the island?"

James grinned. "That would be nice but no. Each of us is issued with a set measure of powder and a regulation number of musket balls. We have to account for them regularly."

Alan asked how much and made a mental note.

"Then why are you bringing the gun if you can't hunt with it?"

"Because he's married to the thing," answered John. "Do you know, he even takes it to bed with him."

The real answer was, as James' sergeant put it, "To make sure those MacDonalds don't get their thieving hands on it," but James was more diplomatic than either John or the sergeant.

"It's simple really. We have to keep our equipment with us at all times to make sure it doesn't get lost."

"That's sensible," agreed Alan. "You wouldn't want to lose that. It must be one of the finest muskets I've seen."

James began to feel proud. "It's the best. It's got a flintlock, not a matchlock, and it's far more reliable."

"Really? Why is that?"

Naively, James explained how a matchlock worked by touching the gunpowder with a glowing fuse, a primitive system which frequently misfired, with a quarter of the shots not going off at all. The new flintlock, on the other hand, ignited the powder with spark and most soldiers preferred it. He went on to say how long it took to reload, how far it could shoot and with what accuracy.

"And look at this," he enthused. He pulled his bayonet from the sheath at his waist and, instead of ramming it down the barrel, demonstrated the new ring fitting which locked it around the outside of the weapon, leaving the muzzle clear to fire.

"Remarkable," said a fascinated Alan.

"Quite," thought John, as memories of Killiecrankie flooded back, the day when his weapon had been one of the many matchlocks which hadn't gone off. And how different it might have been if the redcoats could have had their bayonets already in place before the battle. There hadn't been time to fit them after the first shot.

They arrived on the island and, as they worked on the gravestone manually, Alan continued working on James verbally but got very little from him. Alan was a master of the art of interrogating people without them realising what he was up to and it soon became clear that, while James knew his weaponry, he had no idea what it was intended for.

With the job finished, the three of them rowed back to the shore of Loch Leven, to find Christina waiting for them. She looked different to usual, for she had cut her hair short again. John had asked her at the time why she had done it, hoping she would say that it was to make her less attractive to James and the other soldiers, but she said it was a surprise and he had to be content with that. To him she was still beautiful anyway.

As they disembarked she came forward and presented John with a folded cloth. "Here is my wedding present to you. Christina MacColl's husband must have proper clothes for the wedding, only the best."

John took it and unravelled it. It was a magnificent plaid. He held it round himself with pride. So this was what Christina had been up to at her loom.

"How do I look, James?" he asked.

"It's magnificent. What do you think, Alan?"

Alan was staring at John's back with a puzzled expression on his face.

"Alan?" asked Christina.

He collected his wits together. "What? Och, yes. It's a fine piece of work but ... er ... Christina ... can you explain to me why there's a single black band running through this bit on John's back?"

"It shows that I made the plaid for someone I love. There are only two. My father wore one before he was killed in the war nearly three years ago. I don't know what happened to it but now I've made a second one," she smiled at John, "for my husband."

Alan was troubled by what Christina said but thought it best to keep his mouth tightly shut for the time being. James turned to congratulate John but was surprised at his look.

"John! Are you alright? You don't look very happy at all. Didn't you understand what Christina said?"

"Yes," John answered. "I understood most of it - but if only I hadn't!"

# 16 Betrayal of Trust

## Mealla Earbsa

# 16 Betrayal of Trust

February 11th 1692

This was a day when many men faced dilemmas. Perhaps the one with the smallest problem was Alan. He had been tempted to say something important to Christina but he decided to keep quiet for the time being. He simply made his excuses and resumed his journey, the last visitor to leave that place in peace and safety during the next 24 hours.

For his part, John was horrified and couldn't hide the fact. Christina wanted to know what had upset him so much.

"I'll explain later," he said.

"But can I?" he thought.

How do you tell the girl you are about to marry that you clubbed her father to death? He dumped the plaid in Christina's arms and walked away, unable to face her any more. A confused Christina was left holding her crumpled up handiwork as her beloved departed. Tearfully, she asked James if he understood what was going on. He was equally confused and unable to help.

Yet John's predicament was small compared to the one that faced John Hill, eight miles away in Fort William. The Military Governor sank his face deep into his hands in despair. He simply couldn't believe the orders he had just received from London.

MacIain's oath of allegiance had been declared too late and therefore invalid, though no one had thought to tell MacIain or the 400 folk he represented. Consequently, he and his whole tribe were to be destroyed. Colonel Hill was commanded to order the massacre at once. Two companies of soldiers had already been planted in the glen, actually living with the people. He had only to give the word for the rest of the troops to be in position and for the bloodshed to begin.

For hours, John Hill's conscience wrestled with his duty. Finally he compromised. He passed on the orders (and hopefully the responsibility) to his new deputy, Lieutenant-Colonel Hamilton.

James Hamilton was an ambitious man, anxious to impress the authorities, both those in the army and those in politics. He was also a hard person, reserving a particular dislike for Highlanders. It made him ideal for the job he'd been given. He set to with a relish, eagerly penning orders to his subordinates.

Four hundred men were to march from Fort William to Kinlochleven. From there they would climb over the Devil's Staircase and seal the eastern end of Glencoe, so preventing any escape onto Rannoch Moor. Their journey was over twenty miles, and would have to be completed during the night, but they were soldiers and should be able to manage it. He would lead this detachment himself, on horse naturally. Three hundred soldiers, already camped on the north side of Ballachulish, were to be

Troop movements
to seal off the glen.

Scale:
1 inch = 3 miles

Fort William

Kinlochleven

Devil's Staircase

Loch Leven

Glen Coe

North Ballachulish

Loch Linnhe

N
E
W
S

ferried over to the southern side and enter the glen from the west. With more than two hundred soldiers already in the glen, and a further seven hundred blocking off the only two practical exits, the fortress of Glencoe was about to become a trap.

Once they received these orders, several hundred soldiers would also have to face this clash of conscience and duty. The first was James MacDiarmid.

Two hours after the incident, he was still puzzling over John's reaction to the wedding present. His thoughts took a new turn as he noticed a mounted officer riding over from the Ballachulish ferry. James stood to attention and saluted.

"At last. Someone who seems to know what they are about," grumbled the officer. "I have a dispatch for your commanding officer, Captain Campbell. Where can I find him?"

"He could be in one of several places, sir. Would you like me to guide you to the most likely?"

The rider glanced around at the locals, who were collecting to gawp at him. He felt uncomfortable and the feeble winter light was fading. James' help might come in useful.

"Very well. Can you keep up with me?"

"There's a friend's pony I can borrow, sir. I'll get it now."

Mounted on one of John's ponies, James rode beside the officer.

"That's a peculiar beast," commented the officer. "I've seen pitch black ponies before but never one

with such a vast mane and so much hair on its tail.
I warrant it has the longest hair of any animal I've
seen. Is it local?"

"Oh no, sir. It's a fell pony from the Cumbrian
mountains."

"So this nest of thieves has taken to robbing as
far away as England now have they? Well, that
won't go on much longer."

"No, you misunderstand me, sir. The ponies
aren't stolen. They belong to an Englishman living
where I'm billeted."

This news caused the officer some disquiet.

"Do you mean to tell me that there are other
people, besides MacDonalds, living here?"

"Oh yes, sir. There's the owner of the ponies. He
plans to set up a quarry at the end of the glen.
Then there's a famous Highland bard visiting the
chief and entertaining us all with his poems and
stories. Other ordinary folk have friends and
relatives staying. They are very hospitable so -"

"That will do!" the officer unexpectedly
snapped. "Quit your babbling and take me to
Captain Campbell as you were ordered."

"Yes, sir," acquiesced a surprised James.

An embarrassing silence followed. Why had the
presence of outsiders troubled the officer? James
would dearly have liked to have known more but
he had the sense not to ask.

He was relieved to find Robert Campbell soon
after, playing at cards and drinking at the home of
one of MacIain's sons. The red glow of the

captain's face, set against his grey hair, showed that he had obviously had a few too many and the messenger was reluctant to give him the despatch in front of his hosts. He invited him into a small side room. James had to help his commanding officer to his feet and lead him out. Next door they found Christina doing her regular tasks for MacIain's sick daughter-in-law. She gave James a smile of recognition but Glenlyon mistook it for a smirk at his own drunken condition.

"Wipe that grin off your face!" he exploded.

Christina didn't understand what she'd done wrong but she knew better than to argue. Robert Campbell also resented the humiliation of being held by a common soldier. He shook himself free of James' grip.

"Unhand me!" he shouted.

Unlike Captain Campbell, the other officer was a Lowlander and not bilingual. He had no idea what was being said but he didn't like the atmosphere so, having fulfilled his duty, he left. James moved over to comfort Christina.

Robert Campbell broke the wax seal and opened his instructions. He wasn't quite so drunk that he couldn't read, even in the weak tallow candle light. The full force of his orders penetrated even his dulled mind and he was visibly shaken. He sat down and read them again but there was no mistake. With a moan, he went over to the hole in the wall that passed for a window and stared out at the snow. As he did so, he unwittingly knocked the sheet he'd been reading to the floor and, Christina, hoping to get back into his good books, picked it up and stood behind him, waiting to hand it back.

She waited a long time, while the unhappy figure continued to stare through the window, seemingly unaware that snow was catching and melting on his face and hair. What kind of commands could have such an effect on a man? James peeped over Christina's shoulder and skimmed down the page. No wonder the dispatch officer had been uneasy.

*You are hereby ordered to fall upon the rebels, the MacDonalds of Glencoe, and put all to the sword under seventy. You are to have a special care that the old fox* * *and his sons do upon no account escape your hands. You are to secure all the avenues that no man escape. This you are to put in execution at five of the clock precisely* ** *; and by that time, or very shortly after it, I'll strive to be with you with a stronger party* ......

* MacIain. ** 5 am.

128

Although James had read less than half the instructions, he'd seen enough before his commanding officer shook his head and seemed to come out of his trance. Fortunately, the first thing he focused on was not James, but the orders in Christina's hand. He hastily snatched them away.

"Can you read?" he demanded.

"No, Captain Campbell, she admitted.

It was a pointless question to some one who knew no English and, fortunately, he didn't think to ask James.

"Get rid of this witless girl," barked Glenlyon and kicked them both out.

Christina sobbed pitifully as she sat on John's pony while James led them back through the cold night to their house. She sank her hands into the thick long mane to keep them warm but it gave her little cheer. John's rejection of her special present, coupled with Glenlyon's harsh treatment, was too much for her. As the piercing wind blew snow against her shawl, she felt not just a physical chill but an emotional one as well.

The cold wind even penetrated through the thick red coat of James' uniform but he felt no discomfort. He was too preoccupied by exactly the same conflict of loyalties that Colonel Hill had faced earlier. Duty or conscience? Which was it to be? His duty sickened him. There was no way he was going to execute this girl nor any of the others he lived with. He'd known them little over a week but in that short time they had become good friends.

On the other hand, what else could he do? Should he warn people and, if so, which ones? It would be impossible to inform the whole glen and, even if he could, he would be putting his comrades in danger. Once their hosts found out what was going to happen, they'd murder all the soldiers in sheer self-defence. Perhaps he should warn just a select few but, again, whom? Wouldn't it be easier to tell no-one?

By the time the pair of them arrived home, James still hadn't made up his mind, which was understandable, for nobody should have to make such decisions, let alone an eighteen-year-old. He looked at Christina's face as he helped her gently down from the pony. Her still tearful eyes made her even more beautiful, yet in only a few hours he would be ordered to kill her and not just her. There was the old lady who had looked after him and the young Englishman he'd got friendly with. What was he to do?

# 17 The Blizzard

Na Gaillinn

# 17 The Blizzard

February 12th 1692

It was 4 a.m. John was dressed in James' smart uniform and, had there been any light to see by, he would have looked unusually smart. In contrast, poor James was wearing only his underwear as he lay on his heather bed with his feet bound and his hands tied behind his back.

"Are you sure about this?" whispered John. "It doesn't seem right somehow."

"I'm quite sure," insisted James. "I know what I'm doing."

"Very well," sighed John. "Is there anything else you want to say? It's your last chance."

"Just be quiet and get on with it," hissed James.

Those were his last words, as John went ahead and gagged him. For a final touch, he covered him over with Christina's wedding present, partly because it was the best thing to keep him warm but mainly because John never wanted to see a black band again. Despite her age, Catherine MacDonald regularly slept like a baby and, much to everyone's relief, she continued to do so this morning.

John patted James on the shoulder, Christina kissed him on the forehead and the pair of them slipped quietly to the door. John peeked out. The wind was blowing the snow hard and it was difficult to see far, which was a mixed blessing.

Hopefully their escape would be aided by the poor visibility but, on the other hand, it was extremely cold to be outside for long. Musket in his right hand and Christina's arm in his left, John set off to the Laroch stream a few yards away. The wide yellow lapels of his coat were wrapped across his face to keep the snow off.

"Halt!"

The harsh voice from their left brought John's military training back into play, as he wheeled Christina round and stood to attention.

"MacDiarmid," John stated from behind the lapels, hoping desperately that they wouldn't blow free and reveal his one word lie. Fortunately the light was still poor and the wind from behind them kept the lapels in place whilst blowing snow in the face of their inquisitor.

"I'm taking this young lady to Ballachulish," he went on, his voice sounding as similar to James as he could make it.

The bayonet in front of him, fixed to a loaded and primed musket, glistened in the snowlight.

"The orders said no prisoners."

"Prisoners?" thought John. "What's happening? I'm going to have to come up with a quick answer."

"This one has special information," he insisted.

"What special information?"

"The officer didn't tell me. He simply ordered me to bring the prisoner to him before 5 a.m."

"I suppose you mean the Major who brought the dispatches for Captain Campbell?"

John decided to agree. "That's the one."

Thankfully John wasn't asked for more details. Instead, the other man, a corporal as it turned out, came forward, seized what he could of Christina's hair, and wrenched her head back so that he could look at her face. She was shivering with cold and fear. It stirred up some kind of sympathy in the soldier and he let her go.

"I see. It's the pretty young thing all the men have been talking about," he remarked. "I hope they spare her. Meanwhile, there's not much time. You'd best be on your way. You're fortunate to get the more pleasant duty, MacDiarmid."

"Yes, Corporal," answered John, clueless as to what the man was talking about. He gave Christina a pull and the pair continued on their way.

By the time they reached the Laroch, the snow closed in again. Hidden from anyone's view, they turned left and headed up the stream. It was a steep and narrow climb over the rocks of the slippery gully. Both were hindered by the darkness, and Christina in particular by her long skirt, but they carried on as fast as they could manage. James had warned them to get as far away as possible and to do so as quickly as possible. He had refused to explain why and John's worries grew by the minute.

Why was that corporal up and about so early? Why was his bayonet fixed? Why was his musket primed? His words were ominous too. What did he mean about hoping they spared Christina? What was the less pleasant duty which he hinted about?

134

They had progressed about half a mile and climbed a couple of hundred feet when they stopped for breath. It was bitterly cold and both of them were shivering. They still couldn't see very much but at that moment the wind seemed to carry a familiar sound to John. Was that a gun shot? Two more followed. Yes, it was. They tried to see back down the valley but the blizzard made it almost impossible. John thought he saw a flicker of flame but he couldn't be certain. He suspected he heard a scream as well but it may have been the wind or his imagination. One thing he was sure about, though, was the unmistakable crack of more musketry. He grabbed Christina's arm and they fled on and up.

By the time they reached the head of the valley, it was getting light. The snow had eased off and they looked back the way they had come. As far as they could make out, no-one was following, though the low cloud cover made it hard to be certain. Christina was exhausted and John was not much better. His fingers were so numb they wouldn't bend and, despite his army footwear, he could hardly feel his wet feet. Yet, they both knew they couldn't stay put for long. If they gave in to their exhaustion, they would die of exposure.

With the route all downhill from now on, the going should have been easier. They might even have generated a bit of warmth too, only Christina simply couldn't get started again. John took off his beautiful red army coat and wrapped it around her. In his condition and in that weather, it was an act of real love. Then he picked her up in his arms and carried her on down Glen Duror. Very soon his arms ached. He managed to put her across his shoulders, rather like a fireman's carry and went on like that. It was sheer dogged determination that kept him going as long as he did. He managed five miles, much of it carrying Christina, before he collapsed, frozen and exhausted.

An hour later, and a quarter of a mile further down the glen, a man stepped out of a remote but sizeable house. The wind was sharp but he planned to enjoy some tobacco and absorb the new morning's beautiful snow-covered scenery. Before he could light his pipe, however, he was distracted by a pitiful call from nearby.

It was a strange sight. A dishevelled creature, wrapped in an oversized army coat, was trying to crawl through the snow. Suspiciously, the observer cast his eye about. Was this some kind of a trick? He slipped back into his home in order to peer out a couple of minutes later, carrying a loaded pistol and backed by a couple of armed gillies. The red bundle had moved, though not far. Carefully he approached it, threw back the cover and poked the pistol at the person underneath.

"Christina!"

"Alan!"

# 18 Explanations

Mineadchadh

# 18 Explanations

February 13th 1692

John stumbled from his bed to find Alan brooding by the fire. The sound caused him to turn and make straight for the invalid, his arms out wide and a broad grin across his face.

"John! It's so good to see you up. Man, when we found you, further up the glen, we believed you'd frozen to death. Indeed you would have been were it not for Christina. Once we got you inside and in front of a fire, she spent the next few hours blowing on your hands and feet and rubbing some life back into them. How are you now?"

"I hope I'm not as bad as I feel. Where am I?"

"Enjoying the hospitality of my winter residence. Actually, it doubles up as my spring, summer and autumn ones too."

John was in no mood for wit and interrupted. "Where's Christina?"

"She's in bed asleep. I suspect she'll be staying there with a heavy cold but that's understandable. Would you like to see her?"

John hesitated.

"Later, perhaps. Can I talk to you first, Alan?"

"To me? Since when have I been more important than your wife-to-be? After all you two have been through, I would have thought you'd want each other's company, to sort out your future together."

John was slow to answer. "We don't have one."

Alan was puzzled. "That cold weather has affected your brain. Why-ever not? I know some terrible things must have happened yesterday, but don't let that destroy your plans. When I saw you both a few days ago you were doting on each other. Why, the girl had just made you the most magnificent plaid I've ever seen and you were showing it off," he argued.

Then he remembered John's strange behaviour afterwards.

"But there was something wrong, wasn't there?"

"There certainly was. Alan, I need to share something with someone I can trust. If I talk to you, can I have your assurance that you'll tell no-one else, unless I allow it?"

"You're asking a lot, John. You know little enough about me, so why choose me to take into your confidence?"

"Because I'm talking to the kind man who paid my fare at the ferry, the man who helped me erect Donald MacColl's gravestone, the man who rescued me from the snow - a friend, if I may call you that. I need to unburden myself, and take some advice perhaps, but that's all. But, please, I must stress that it goes no further than you for the present. Is anyone else within earshot?"

"Aye, my gillies, but they have no English. If it's a personal matter, go ahead. I'm very good at listening."

"Thank you, Alan. I'll keep this simple. I was at Killiecrankie, though not on the Highlanders' side."

Alan raised an eyebrow but didn't interrupt.

"I killed a man there and escaped wrapped in my victim's plaid, a beautifully made cloth but with one peculiar characteristic - a single black band running through it. It's a long story, but I ended up as the guest of Donald MacColl. No one knew about the plaid, for by that time I'd got rid of it. Anyhow, as you are aware, I fell hopelessly in love with Christina. She loved me and naturally enough I wanted to wed the girl. Everything was fine until I tried on that cursed garment she made me. You noticed the black band didn't you? You asked her what it was for and she told us how she had made one like it for her father."

There was a long pause as John braced himself to continue. It was some time before he could go on.

"Alan, can you see my predicament? That sweet child loves me, not knowing I'm the one who orphaned her. What am I going to say?"

Alan drummed his fingers on the arm of his chair for a few moments before committing himself to an answer.

"Might I suggest that you say nothing, at least not yet? First let me tell you a story from Killiecrankie."

"You mean you were there too? Which side? Oh Alan!"

Alan smirked. "I said I had a story from the place. I didn't say I was there."

"Now you're talking like Patrick O'Shea."

"Nonsense. We don't even have the same accent."

"How would you know?"

"Know what?"

"How would you know anything about Patrick O'Shea?" John insisted, having caught Alan at his own game.

"You must have mentioned him at some time."

"Oh yes? When? What did I say?"

"Och, I can't remember now. It's of no consequence."

"Oh yes, it is. Alan," John stared straight into his eyes, "we have to be straight with each other or not at all."

This was awkward. Alan wondered whether what he himself knew was worth the information which John had. Perhaps it was.

"Alright, but can I, in turn, have your assurance that anything I say goes no further?"

John shrugged. "Exchange is no robbery."

"Very well. Patrick O'Shea was a soldier in Kenmuir's regiment at Killiekrankie, was he not?"

"Yes," John agreed.

"He escaped with a wound to his arm and rejoined his regiment under cover of darkness. Did you know that?"

"I knew about the wound and I know that he planned to rejoin."

"Well, that's what he did but he decided, soon after, that he'd had enough after all. Then, in his own words, a miracle occurred, when some back pay appeared. Patrick complained that it wasn't much but by some skilful card playing with other soldiers who had also received such pay, he won more than enough to buy a passage on a ship to the Americas. You'll understand that he was not the sort of man to quit the army in the regulation manner, however, so he needed my help in order to be on his way. For a certain sum of money, I arranged matters for him. There, does that satisfy you?"

Alan hoped it would, as John mulled over what he had heard. Although it was the truth it wasn't the whole truth. Patrick O'Shea had actually been one of Alan's Jacobite accomplices, though there was no way that Alan would have given that away. Patrick worked from within the very ranks of the Government army itself. He had thought himself safe in battle, having a secret badge, the white-coloured patch used to repair the tear in his left sleeve, together with a special code word and hand signals. Members of Dundee's forces knew about these and knew to leave be any such red coat they came across. The worst that would happen would be for him to be taken prisoner before conveniently being allowed to "escape" later on.

It had all gone adrift at Killiekrankie when an arrow, which didn't know the rules, not only hit him but scored a bulls eye on the white patch. It destroyed most of it and Patrick's own blood soon dyed the rest more or less the same colour as the coat. John had no idea about any of this.

"All right," he conceded. "I'll accept what you say. Now tell me the rest."

"A few days before Killiekrankie, King James' army was joined by what I can best describe as "irregulars", men with no special allegiance but who got involved for the excitement and the thought of plunder. There was one who used the name "MacGeil" though I believe it was a false one. "MacGregor" may have been nearer the truth but the name has been outlawed and to use it carries a heavy penalty. No matter, whoever he was, he struck up some kind of friendship with the men of Glencoe and that evening he ended up playing cards with them.

"Few folk had actual coins to wager so they used things instead, a kind of gambling by barter, and during the game, MacGeil, who was dressed in little more than rags, won a plaid and a quantity of whisky.

"The MacDonald who lost the garment had not only been reluctant to part with it but I understand that he also had a violent reputation. MacGeil, fearful of what might happen in the night, decided it would be sensible to take his winnings and join up with the Appin Stewarts for a while. He got drunk, became a nuisance and was told to go away. He certainly did that, for he wasn't seen again till after the battle. He must have polished off all the spirits at the same time for, when he was found next day, about half a mile from the field, he was hardly conscious. He was also naked, apart from bits of a Government army uniform."

John, eyes closed, was shaking his head.

"You're making this up to keep me happy. Patrick said he was dead."

143

"Patrick O'Shea was never a good judge of people. I am not making this up. I can find a dozen men to verify the story. I could probably find MacGeil himself if you like."

"No, please. I don't think I want to meet him again."

"Huh, I thought not. I don't suppose he's forgiven you for the sore head you gave him but never mind. He doesn't know that you were responsible. He reckoned that he'd been robbed of the best plaid he'd ever had by the Glencoe MacDonalds, who must have ambushed him and taken it back. He went on to say that, if ever he met any of them again, he'd keep an eye out, for he'd recognise that plaid anywhere. It had an unmistakable feature."

John grinned for the first time.

"Might that feature be a single black band?" he enquired.

"It might," Alan grinned back.

"So you're saying that it wasn't me who killed Christina's father. In fact I haven't killed anyone. Praise God! I can marry Christina after all. Oh Alan, how can I ever thank you?"

Alan gave John an impish look.

"Well, to remind you of part of your tale which you left out, you could begin by reimbursing me for the clothes, the three sovereigns and the food you stole during my swim at Loch Rannoch. I'm not a mean man so I'll let you off the mouthful of wine."

# 19 Update

*Nuadhaich*

# 19 Update

March 5th 1692

John stared out to sea. How ironic that, two weeks ago, it was his turn to stand on the shore watching, while Christina left in a boat. Two and a half years before, it had been the other way round and at least on that occasion he had had an idea of where she was. Her departure seemed an age ago yet Alan's words were still so vivid.

"I'm arranging this for your good," he had said. "There's the possibility that patrols are searching the countryside for the pair of you even now, and the further you are from this place, the less you will be at risk."

"And less likely to attract attention to me," he could have added.

"John, we'll need to destroy this uniform. It invites too many questions. I'll give you some of my Lowland clothes to wear. I've reason to believe that my garments fit you," he winked.

"Now, there's a fellow down in Appin whom I can persuade to take the three of us south, by boat, as far as Easedale. It's a small island between Mull and the mainland where you should feel at home. It has a well established quarry, digging almost identical slates to the Glencoe ones. Why, they even have the fool's gold in them!"

Once there, Alan dropped a bombshell. John was to stay there and work for his keep, while

Alan took Christina on to a destination he refused to disclose.

"This coastline borders Campbell country," he had explained. "That's why we didn't come overland but by boat, even in February. As a visiting Sassenach, you'll not be linked with whatever happened in Glencoe but, with Christina, it's different. She needs to be well clear of this region."

"But surely you can take me too?"

"Sorry, I can't. The boat sails on with a cargo of slates. There'll not be room for you as well so just stay here and work around the place to earn your keep until I return. The folk will be glad of a strong young man who knows what he's doing."

It was a brief rebuff and John had to accept it. However, it wasn't the true reason Alan had left him behind. The truth was that Alan's work in the Jacobite cause had created in him a very suspicious nature. While he wanted to believe that John was sincere, one or two incidents left him in some doubt and needed clearing up first. Was it just a coincidence that this Englishman had settled in with the Glencoe folk shortly before the soldiers arrived? On his own admission he'd fought in their army before. Could he still be serving them secretly, doing for William's Government what Patrick O'Shea had done for the Jacobites? It seemed a little too convenient that he'd been allowed to escape, just before the killing started. Had this man secretly paved the way for all this? If he had, it was worrying, for he now knew something of Alan's own activities. Alan had left, intending to sort out these and many other questions.

Weeks later, John's mind was still fixed on these matters as he vainly scoured the boatless southern seascape.

"Do all Sassenachs spend more time looking at the sea than working?"

The voice brought John abruptly back into the present.

"Alan! How did you get here? I've been watching the sea for days and didn't see the boat."

"You wouldn't. I came a different route, from the Isle of Seil, and crossed the sound to the north of here. Men don't always return the way they leave."

John wasn't interested in that.

"Where is Christina? Haven't you brought her with you?"

"Regrettably for you, young sir, no. I found her a position as a housemaid with a family of fine folk who take good care of her. Mind you, she and the other housemaid spend so much time debating matters of religion, that the two of them do less work than the one did on her own."

"Well, if Christina is doing a lot of talking with someone, she's still somewhere in the Highlands or Islands."

Alan considered John's logic and inwardly smiled before moving the conversation on.

"Aye, she's settled among friends but that's enough of womenfolk. There's some men's talk that's called for. Let's enjoy a seat by the shore."

They watched the icy waves lapping the cold black stones though John wasn't concerned with their chilly surroundings. What did Alan want to talk about?

"I'm sorry I've been away so long," Alan began. "I've been finding out a few things and I'll share with you what I can but, first, tell me what you remember of your last hours in Glencoe."

"There isn't a lot to tell but, if it's of any interest, where would you like me to start?"

"How about when I left Laroch?"

"All right. It was a cold afternoon and I spent the time indoors with the others around the peat fire. I wasn't very sociable. I was busy trying to think what to say to Christina. She wasn't there by the way. She appeared about four hours later, when James MacDiarmid brought her back from John MacIain's house. She was still crying, at the way I rejected her present I supposed, and I still couldn't face her. It was a relief when James immediately invited me outside for a talk. I expected to get a telling-off for the way I had treated Christina but it was nothing like that at all.

"He stated that Christina and I were in danger, though he refused to say how, and that the only way we could escape was to tie and gag him so that it looked like he had been overpowered. Then I was to leave, dressed in his uniform, at a ridiculous hour in the morning, taking Christina along as a supposed prisoner. At first, I thought he was fooling with me but he was deadly serious. He insisted that

Christina and I should do this so that, when the danger appeared, we'd already be gone. James would be released, unharmed, by his comrades. We were to say nothing to anybody else."

"Not even Catherine?"

"James said that she would be safe because he would say she was over seventy. She wasn't, but even if she had been, I didn't understand what that had to do with it. Honestly, Alan, this is as much as I know, though I've no doubt you know more than me by now."

Alan knew a great deal more. He had lots of contacts and in many places, for his information was detailed.

"James MacDiarmid saved you and Christina from a horrific slaughter. There's those who would argue that MacIain's people had this coming to them sooner or later. We Highlanders are no strangers to retaliation, and I would agree that the Glencoe folk had earned some for all the trouble they'd caused, but not like this." Alan shook his head. "It's beyond belief."

"What is?"

"Trusted guests getting up in the night and murdering their hosts."

"Surely they didn't!"

"Surely they did. Those soldiers received their orders for the massacre right from the highest authority. Dutch William's signature was found at both the beginning and the end of the document. The details were planned by lesser men of course.

The Secretary of State for Scotland was involved, along with Campbell of Breadalbane and probably the Earl of Argyll, since it was his regiment that did the dirty work.

"It would have happened even earlier had it not been for Colonel Hill at Fort William. He was winning folks' trust and believed that we Jacobite clans would accept the new monarchy peacefully. He did everything he could to put off signing the orders to his men but in the end his duty as a soldier overruled his personal feelings. I fear he'll regret this whole affair for the rest of his life.

"Indeed, this has been a story of intrigue, of dark dealings going on behind closed doors, men risking their lives, listening at windows, searching secret documents, discovering wicked truths ..."

151

"Alan. Spare the drama. I want the facts."

Alan looked sorely disappointed. "Very well. Let's forget great men and come back to you. I've news which concerns acquaintances of yours."

John leaned forward, beginning to feel the cold.

"I'm told that a soldier by the name of MacDiarmid was billeted with a lady called Catherine MacDonald. The house was also occupied by one John Clerk and his fiancée. During the night before the massacre, MacDiarmid bound and gagged Clerk before deserting. His motive appeared to be Clerk's fiancée, with whom he absconded. Whether it was with her connivance or whether he kidnapped her is not known. Nor is it known whether either of the pair survived the blizzard. There's a warrant out for MacDiarmid's arrest, just in case."

"One moment, Alan. That can't be right. When they released the bound man he would have told them something different."

"They didn't release him. John, tell me exactly how you left James."

John shrugged his shoulders.

"The way I said. He was trussed up on his bed and he had my plaid over him to keep warm."

Alan's voice sounded grave.

"I fear the plaids which Christina weaves must be cursed. Being wrapped in that one was his undoing."

Alan took John's arm.

"Brace yourself for some bad news. In the weak early morning light, the soldiers who entered the house simply saw a figure under a blanket. He couldn't cry out, he wasn't recognised and they shot him."

John was devastated. He didn't know what to say and a long silence followed. Finally he spoke.

"How about Angus?"

"He was last seen sheltering behind a low bank, torn between whether to escape with his wife and baby or to fight his way through the soldiers to rescue his father. No one has seen any of them since."

"And Catherine?"

"She's dead too. I'm sorry. The orders required the execution of all under seventy, which explains what James said to you, but James never had a chance to do anything."

John still couldn't accept it.

"Alan, even with your explanation, this doesn't make sense. Someone must have recognised James when they came to clear up."

"Apparently not. The only clearing up the redcoats did was to remove one thousand four hundred cows, five hundred horses and hundreds of sheep and goats* plus any money or household items they could find. It was left for the refugees to return and bury their dead and James wasn't wearing his uniform," - Alan's look was almost accusing - "You were. I don't know, you seem to spend all your time swapping clothes back and

* Figures taken from MacDonald claims for compensation during later enquiry. Government figures were a fraction of this. Readers can form their own opinions on where the truth lay.

forth, first from a soldier to a Highlander at Killiecrankie, from a Highlander to a Lowlander at Loch Rannoch and then from a civilian to a soldier again at Glencoe. Have you ever thought of a career on the stage?"

"There's more to it than that. We may have swapped places. We couldn't swap faces."

"Poetry as well, John. My, you are talented."

"Alan, don't fool with me. Murder is a serious matter, especially when it's on my account."

Alan gave a deferential tilt of his head.

"Sorry, John. Forgive me for being cynical. It's the only way I know of coping with what I've had to do lately. Still, I see you're in no mood for it. Do you want me to go on?"

"Not particularly but my mind won't be at rest until I know what happened. Why didn't someone realise who James really was? The gag wasn't big enough to hide his whole face and the pair of us look totally different."

Alan paused. He was having trouble getting out the words but finally he managed it.

"James was shot in the head. Come now, John. You've been a soldier. You must know the damage a lead ball does at close range. He was unrecognisable."

It took John some time for all this to sink in. He questioned every possible weakness in Alan's account but got nowhere. The information came from several reliable sources, so it must have happened, but John didn't want to believe it. Not

James, not that cheerful teenager, so good-natured, so helpful, so likeable, so innocent - it wasn't fair. John burst into tears and at that point Alan accepted he was genuine.

There was silence for a while, punctuated only by John's sobs, then Alan grew philosophical.

"Alasdair MacIain once told me how grateful he was that we Appin Stewarts occupied the territory between him and clan Campbell. He had little love for them and, till now, I felt the same. Yet MacDiarmid is a Campbell name and when I think about James ... aye well, I don't know what to think."

"Christina and I owe our lives to him," sniffed John, "but there's not much we can do about it now."

He thought a bit then wiped his eyes. He'd had an idea.

"Unless I could make him a memorial stone, you know, like I did for Donald MacColl. Look at all these massive stones. I could start right now. Would you like to help me erect another one, Alan?"

Alan shook his head.

"That's not advisable, John. No, don't interrupt. Listen to me. I understand how you feel but James MacDiarmid has to remain an uncaptured deserter. John Clerk must remain dead and Christina MacColl must not return to the area. Only you and I know the truth. For your own well-being, you need to start a new life."

"It's a bit rough on James."

"Too true. Labelled a deserter, believed to be a kidnapper, unrecognised for having given his own life in place of two others, dumped in an unmarked grave on his traditional enemies' burial isle - it's the complete opposite of what he deserved but I believe, John, that he would want us to leave it that way. If any of us gives the game away now, his sacrifice could be a complete waste of time."

# 20 Born Again

# A Bhreith A Rithist

# 20 Born Again

May 1st 1692

Alan had disappeared yet again, refusing to say where he was headed, what he would be doing or when he would be back. Moreover, he hadn't restored Christina to her longing sweetheart either. John was left cutting Easedale slates while he waited. One morning, as he paused to wipe the sweat from his face, he noticed a man, not dressed as a local, examining the rocks.

"If he's a dealer come to buy slates, he's come to the wrong end of the island," thought John. "He'll need to talk to the men over towards the ferry."

He rested on his pick, still wondering who the visitor might be, when the man took off his tricorn hat and waved it.

"John!" he called and immediately John recognised the voice.

"Matthew!" he shouted back and, dropping his pick, leapt over the rocks to meet him.

After a welcoming embrace, John had to ask the obvious question, even though he suspected he knew the answer.

"What are you doing here?"

"Looking for you, young man, and right glad I am to have found you. Hannah and I have been worried sick since you left and then I heard about Glencoe. It was hard not to hear about it, really. The Jacobites made sure the news spread everywhere and I doubt there's a corner of the British Isles that doesn't know. It's causing a lot of embarrassment in high places, they say, but that didn't concern me. I only knew that I had to come and find you.

"I got as far as Dumbarton, only to find that Andrew and most of the household were away in Edinburgh. Only Janet was left when I arrived. I was unsure whether to stay and wait for Andrew, for I value his counsel, or whether to press on. Then a miracle occurred. I came across a fellow by the name of Alan Stewart. He was on some kind of business but he didn't elaborate much."

"No," interjected John. "He wouldn't. I guess he asked you a lot about yourself though?"

"Now you come to mention it, yes, he did. Interesting man. Well, anyway, when he found whom I was looking for, he said that, by coincidence, he'd come across you on this very island and that you'd never even got as far as Glencoe."

"He said that, did he?"

"Yes he did and how I praised the Lord for his mercy towards you."

With that he gave John a big hug.

"Well, Matthew. I'm not sure what to say. I suppose you could do with some food. It's about noon and I'm hungry as well. Come, I'll take you back to my lodgings and we can talk further."

John's hosts, a quarrying family, could get by in English and were delighted to meet Matthew. His lowland background, his religion and politics all

159

came second to the fact he was a friend of John's. Towards the end of the meal, they told Matthew what a fine worker John was and how in less than two months he had cut more slate than any other strong young man would in four.

John suddenly choked on his piece of bread. It was all put on as a diversion because he didn't want Matthew and his hosts comparing dates. Nevertheless, the ruse worked and the lady of the house brought him some water while another patted his back.

"Thank you. I'm alright now. I think some fresh air might help. Matthew, would you like to see the rest of the island? It's not very big but it's a fascinating place."

"That sounds good." Turning to his hosts he asked, "Is that alright?"

The family was quite happy and the pair of them set off. Out of earshot, John came to the point.

"I didn't really choke on my bread, Matthew."

"No. You were never a very good actor, John."

"The reason was that I had to kill the conversation. You could have landed me in an awkward situation. Look, Matthew, I haven't been here all the time."

"No?"

"No. I was told not to let on about ... oh, what does it matter? Listen."

John gave Matthew a brief rundown of his circumstances. Despite Alan's warning, he told him that he had been in Glencoe after all but how he and

Christina had escaped. Matthew took a deep breath once John had finished.

"That's an amazing story. You certainly seem to keep your guardian angel busy these days."

John nodded in agreement. He had little else to add so Matthew carried on.

"So what happens now John? You're free to stay here, I suppose. Free to move on elsewhere perhaps. You are more than welcome to come back with me. What are you going to do?"

John was not as enthusiastic as he would once have been.

"I don't know Matthew. You use the word 'free' and in a sense I am and yet," he shook his head, "and yet, deep inside, I just don't feel it."

Matthew sat himself on a convenient rock in the sunshine, seeming to watch the waves lapping on the rocks, but really taking the pressure off John by not talking directly at him.

"Do you want to talk about it?" he asked.

John sat next to him, also looking at the waves.

"Yes, Matthew. I'd like that. It's simple, really. My life resembles one of those waves. I don't know where the waves come from and I don't know where I came from either. I do know, however, that each wave has come a long way and so have I. Yet, what happens to a wave? It ends up breaking on these rocks and it's forgotten, assuming anyone noticed it in the first place. Am I going to end up like that?

"My wondering began when I started teaching myself more Gaelic, using some books Alan lent me.

He has an interesting selection. He was educated in France, I'm told. Do you know, he's fluent in Gaelic, English, and French and even had some Latin and Greek books. I could only carry a small number so I decided to find a Gaelic book and see if I could find an English version. I thought that, if I read a sentence in English, and then repeated it in Gaelic, I might learn a bit faster. Would you believe it? There was only one book in Gaelic, the Bible. The Gaelic one is the first of its kind, printed only a couple of years ago. In some ways I'm surprised to find Alan has a copy. It doesn't seem his sort of book ... sorry, I'm getting off the subject, aren't I? We're talking about me, not Alan. Coming back to my study, I don't how much Gaelic it taught me but I learned a lot about myself."

Matthew was all ears as John went on.

"Take that parable about the prodigal son. There's a bit where the son says to his father, 'I have sinned both against Heaven and against you.' I've done the same haven't I? I've cleared matters up with you but I haven't put things right with God and, you know, Matthew, I get terrible feelings of guilt about the past. I've thought about the ten commandments and I haven't done too well in keeping them. I've got myself into so many scrapes that I've had to lie, rob and nearly kill to get out of them. How does a person like me make amends with God? Have I gone too far?"

Matthew took his gaze off the waves, turned his head and smiled brightly at John.

"People have prayed and waited many years to hear you talk like this. Tell me, have you been as bad as the criminal on the cross next to Jesus? Have you persecuted innocent Christians, as the apostle Paul did? Of course not and if they could find God's forgiveness so can you."

"I don't see how. I've still got so much to answer for."

Matthew leaned back on his rocky seat and scratched his head before coming up with a suggestion.

"King William seemed to think you had a lot to answer for, too, when his soldiers were supposed to have disposed of you, a couple of months back. Yet you're still alive. How come?"

John thought about it for a bit.

"I suppose it's because someone else died, instead of me."

"That's right," confirmed Matthew. "You went free, even though your death sentence was carried out, simply because it was carried out on another person. As far as the law is concerned, John Clerk was executed on Saturday the 13th of February, 1692, at a place called Glencoe - despite the fact that he's sitting talking to me right now.

"God sees you in a similar light. John Clerk was executed more than one and a half thousand years ago, at a place called Calvary. James MacDiarmid took your place where a king's law was concerned. Jesus did the same for you where God's laws were concerned. You can go free in both cases."

"I still don't feel it."

"Of course not. You haven't done anything about it, have you?"

"Haven't I? No, I suppose not."

John looked pensively at Matthew but only until a realisation crossed his face and a determined look replaced it.

"Right. That's going to change. Matthew, close your eyes; it's my turn to lead the prayers."

Matthew listened sensitively as John came to God and admitted he'd done much to offend Him. He regretted all those things and asked that, because Jesus had taken his place, God would no longer hold him answerable. He ended by putting his whole future at God's disposal.

"Amen!" shouted Matthew.

John grinned. He was going to have to get used to Matthew's sort because he'd become one himself. This was a new beginning.

"It's a fresh start, Matthew. My life began in obscurity but now it feels like it's begun all over again, but with a meaning this time. It's like being, I don't know, like being born again I suppose."

"Try reading the Gospel of John chapter three and verse three in that Gaelic Bible," said Matthew. "If Jesus didn't use exactly those words, find yourself a better translation to learn from."

# 21 Plans for the Future

# An Plan A Tha Ri Teachd

# 21 Plans for the Future

May 1st 1692

That afternoon, John showed Matthew around the little island. There wasn't much more to see and they ended up chatting.

"That sorry affair at Glencoe must have put paid to your plans for a quarry at Ballachulish, John. I can't see you returning there. What will you do instead, stay here?"

"Possibly but I have a more important matter on my mind. Matthew, both you and your cousin are leaders in your own churches. Would either of you be willing to conduct a wedding ceremony for Christina and myself?"

"It's flattering to be asked, John, but I'm not sure that one of us could."

"Why not?"

"I'm not sure that you match spiritually."

"Pardon?"

"Is she a Christian?"

"Well, near enough," answered John guardedly.

"Hmm," mused Matthew. "You could once have said that of Andrew's maid, Janet, but it was only a name. When you last saw her, it had become more than that, hadn't it? You must have seen the difference. How does Christina compare?"

John thought of the mixture of superstition rolled up with bits of Christianity that made up Christina's beliefs. Then he considered Janet,

166

whose sour tongue would once have cut a person to shreds in seconds and who could inflict more damage on a man using her broomstick than a Highlander might with a broadsword. Yet how she'd changed since becoming a Christian.

"Well, not like Janet, perhaps."

"So, in simple English, she would call herself a Christian but in reality, she isn't, not like you or Janet."

"Well ..."

"John, I'll be blunt. A Christian should only marry another Christian. The Bible is quite clear about that, not because the God who wrote it wants to spoil our happiness. He says it for our good."

John made no reply. He knew he'd regret it if he did. Instead, he got up, grabbed the pickaxe he'd forgotten earlier on and went off to let his feelings loose on the slates. He felt angry enough to smash up the whole island at first but, once his energy had almost gone, though not his rage, he went for a walk. He was furious with God, the Bible and Matthew's understanding of it. The Almighty was on the receiving end of a string of complaints. John began by telling God that He wasn't fair.

"I gave my life to You and the first thing You do is deny me the wife I've been through so much to win."

He went on to tell God just what he thought about the whole business, kicked a few stones and sulked. After a while he calmed down. He hadn't been struck by lightning or anything like that yet, so what was God thinking?

He turned back and found Matthew, still in the same spot and obviously waiting for him. John perched himself on an outcrop just above Matthew, in order to gain a psychological advantage before firing the loaded question he'd thought up.

"How can robbing me of the person I love be for my good?"

"God isn't a robber. He cares about you and Christina far more than you will ever realise. Oh, John, how can I explain things?

"Look at it like this. Life is like a journey, a tough one at times, and we need companions to help us through it. As children, we needed older folk to get us started on our way but when a child becomes a man or a woman it's different. We still need company to support us through our journey but usually parents and guardians have to make way for a new companion, a husband or wife.

"The couple travel together, supporting and encouraging each other until one of them reaches the end of the journey.

"God has mapped out your future but Christina doesn't have your beliefs. Until she does, you're not even starting from the same point, you'll want to follow different paths and you certainly don't have the same destination. You'll either end up coming apart or you'll follow her away from the way you ought to go."

"It doesn't have to be like that," John protested. "I don't have to follow her. If my way is correct, why can't I direct her along my path?"

Matthew didn't give John a straight answer. Instead, he complained that he was feeling stiff and asked John for a hand to help him rise. John didn't stop to think what an odd request this was from someone as fit as Matthew and offered his hand. Matthew gripped it firmly and yanked John down from his perch.

"What are you doing?" demanded an angry John, as he got back to his feet.

"Answering your question. It's easier for Christina to pull you down from your faith than it is for you to pull her up to yours. I know from experience. I've seen many people get married, intending to change their spouse afterwards. I've seen none achieve it and I care about you too much to help you join their number."

John felt unable to continue. He suspected Matthew was right but he was reluctant to admit it so he changed the subject.

"I'll think about what you say but let's leave this spot for bit, Matthew. I need to do something different. How about going fishing?" he suggested. "Archie, our host's neighbour, has a boat that he'll lend us."

Matthew went with Archie to get the boat while John collected his thoughts, as well as the fishing tackle. As he approached the boat, he found Matthew and Archie talking with the ferryman and two others whom he'd clearly just landed. There was a mixture of English and Gaelic and not everyone seemed to understand each other.

"John," called Matthew. "Your friend Alan has just come off the ferry with this pretty young lady. I don't know her name but apparently she's cousin Andrew's new housemaid. I don't suppose you've met her?"

John could only see the visitor's back but, as she turned round, he was presented with her face.

"Met her?" he asked with surprise. "I want to marry her!"

# 22 The New Christina

# An Cairistìona Nuadh

# 22 The New Christina

May 1st 1692

Rather than feel excited at Christina's reappearance, John felt cross. How was he going to explain things to her at this point? He rounded on Alan.

"Would you tell me what's happening? You informed me that Christina was in the Highlands or Islands and now I hear that she's been in Dumbarton and Edinburgh all this time, where I could have kept her company. I thought I could trust you."

Alan looked hurt, though he had trouble hiding a slight curl in his lips.

"Well, there's a fine welcome. I return the delight of your life to you and all the thanks I get is accusations of mistrust. I'll take her off to another island if you prefer but I thought you were missing her. Anyway, I never said she was where you thought."

"You said she was speaking Gaelic to the other housemaid and where else do housemaids speak Gaelic other than ... other than ... Oh ... of course."

"Other than a certain house in Dumbarton? Was that what you were going to say?"

"You mean Janet was the other housemaid. It was Andrew's household you talked about?"

"It was." Alan chuckled at the trick he'd played on John. "Janet has not forgotten her mother

172

tongue and I told you no untruth, despite your accusations."

"But you told me one," butted in Matthew. "You said that John had been here all the time when he'd really been ...."

"Excuse me interrupting," intervened Alan. "I see you are off fishing. Let me come with you and we'll give Archie a break. We'll clear up any misunderstandings once we're out in the boat."

"You can take my place as well," added John. "I need to talk to Christina, alone preferably, but I'll help you launch the boat first."

As soon as the boat was clear of the rocks, and also out of earshot, Alan explained to Matthew why he had misled him.

"I believe we need to keep John's presence in Glencoe under wraps for some time yet. That's why I interrupted you on the shore. His life could still be at risk. So could Christina's."

Matthew shook his head and sighed.

"I can't accept lying, although I accept that you meant well by it. I'll make no more of the matter. I hope you haven't misled me on anything else."

"Not a thing," answered Alan, truthfully for once. Not that he could have said the same to many other folk, had they asked him. He'd spent the last few weeks leaving printed sheets, spiced with rumours and innuendoes about the Glencoe massacre, around the taverns, coffee houses and other gossip centres of Glasgow and Edinburgh. He even joined in the talk, helping to exaggerate the stories and showing King William and his supporters in a very bad light.

Meanwhile, both Christina and John looked glumly at each other. John forced a smile and beckoned with his hand. Christina returned a very synthetic smile of her own, hardly what you'd expect from two lovers reunited after such a long spell and she followed him a short distance. John wasn't sure what to say in English, let alone Gaelic, as he glanced back to the girl he was about to disappoint. Fortunately, she spoke first.

"I learn English."

John forgot his problems for a few moments, amazed to hear her use his language for the first time. He sat down on a slate outcrop, grasped her hand and sat her down beside him.

"That's marvellous. Did Janet teach you?"

Christina looked awkward and raised her free hand.

"I understand not. Speak slowly."

"It ... is ... good. Is ... Janet ... your ... teacher?"

"Ah," she nodded. "Is Janet, my teacher."

John grinned at her mix of English words and Gaelic grammar. He was wondering whether it should be called Englic or Gaelish but dropped those thoughts as she turned away to look down at the ground. Her limited foray into English was exhausted, as she lapsed back into her own tongue.

"John, I love you but," she pulled her hand free, "but we cannot marry."

Neither could look each other in the eye.

"I know," confirmed John, staring straight ahead. Was she going to wallop him again? He braced himself but, if anything, there was a hint of surprise, not anger, in her voice.

"Who told you?"

"Matthew."

She looked puzzled. "How does Matthew know?" she asked. "Only Janet, Andrew and I know."

John was confused and he knew it wasn't his Gaelic.

"Let's begin again," he suggested. "What do you, Janet and Andrew know?"

"About my new life. Look."

She pulled a folded piece of paper from the leather pouch around her neck. John wondered what it was. She used to keep lucky charms in there. Was this another one?

"I can't read," explained Christina, "but you can. Janet asked me to give you this and tell you to read it from the Bible. She said it's possible you would understand."

John glanced up from the note. It definitely was not a lucky charm.

"I don't need to look in a Bible. I know John chapter three and verse three in English and in Gaelic. 'Born again.' Is that you?"

"It is. I thought I was a Christian but it was only a name. Janet explained things to me. Today, I am a real Christian."

John could hardly contain himself any longer. There would be a lot of sorting out, a lot of explanations, so much to do but the future looked grand. He just had to tell Christina the good news. His intentions were thwarted however as, at that very moment, Matthew and Alan came into view in the boat.

"Ahoy there!" shouted an excited Matthew. "Two minutes out from land and we rowed straight into a shoal of herring. Look how many we caught. Are you hungry?"

"No, I'm not!" John shouted back. "You are interrupting an important conversation. Go away."

He turned to explain to Christina, when another thought struck him. He called back after the boat instead.

"Hey, you in the boat! About that wedding ...."

# Epilogue

Although this is a made up adventure, the historical and geographical settings are real. Here is what really happened following these events.

Many MacDonalds returned to Glencoe. Most of them, including MacIain's sons, had escaped. The attempt to annihilate failed, for three main reasons.

Firstly, the eastern entrance to the glen from Rannoch Moor, wasn't sealed off in time. The soldiers had had a fourteen mile overnight march to Kinlochleven, contending with a blizzard as they went. Arriving cold and tired, there was no way they could manage the six mile climb over the Devil's Staircase, the pass at the eastern edge of the Aonnach Eagach Ridge. They sheltered as best they could until the weather eased. Even then they couldn't get going for two lieutenants, on hearing their orders, were too disgusted to obey them. A further delay followed as several men had to arrest their own officers. When they finally reached their objective, it was 11 am, several hours too late.

Secondly, the soldiers sent to seal the western entrance also arrived too late, though this appears to have been deliberate. Major Duncanson, the officer commanding this part of the operation clearly instructed Captain Campbell to begin at *five* a.m., yet records show that his own orders actually said *seven* a.m. Whatever his motive for altering the orders, the result was the same - the soldiers at the western end also appeared on the scene more or less after the deed was done.

The third, and most significant, reason lay with the soldiers actually billeted in Glencoe. Like their hosts, the bulk of the guests were Highlanders too, and hospitality was equally as sacred to both sides. When the time came to break the trust, friendships even, that had formed between them all, the soldiers just could not do it. They were struck by some kind of temporary deafness and blindness. They chose not to hear the terrified breathing behind the wall. Their shots flew pathetically wide of the fleeting shadows. Less than forty were killed, meaning they allowed nine out of ten of their victims to escape.

The massacre should have been a warning to the men of Glencoe but they persisted in their warlike ways until 1746. At Culloden, the last land battle in Britain, the redcoats' bayonets did what John Clerk and his fellow soldiers at Killiecrankie hadn't been able to. They stopped a Highland charge. It was the end of an era.

John's unfulfilled ambition in the story eventually occurred. Men from Easedale settled at Ballachulish and developed the quarry there.

The Easedale quarries themselves were dealt a death blow at the end of the nineteenth century, when a powerful Atlantic storm flooded the workings. They never fully recovered.

During the land clearances of the early 1800's,

greedy people in power replaced the human population of the Highlands with more economically attractive sheep. Whole populations were forced to leave the Highlands in their droves, and driven overseas to places like Canada and America or even Australia and New Zealand, but the Ballachulish slate quarries provided an occupation which allowed thousands of other folk to remain. The workings carried on into the twentieth century but, like Easedale, those at Ballachulish have themselves fallen silent.

Today, thousands of holidaymakers visit the areas mentioned in this story. On the fields of Killiecrankie, where the Highlanders once routed King William III's forces, only sheep dogs chase around these days. Tourists picnic on the garnet shores between Loch Rannoch and Coillie Dhu, one of the few natural woodlands left. They even sit under ancient trees that were growing there at the time of this story.

Glencoe itself has been opened up by a major trunk road passing through it. Those who stop off at Ballachulish will find a black band there but nothing to do with one a young woman wove for good luck. Much good that did Colin MacColl, a man who called himself MacGeil or James MacDiarmid. No, sandwiched between lighter rocks runs the dark slate, the one worthwhile black band in Glencoe, put there by John and Christina's Maker.

# What happened to them?

Just as the places and events in this story were real, so were many of the characters. Readers of earlier manuscripts wanted to know more about them, so here are brief biographical details.

**Campbell,** Captain Robert of Glenlyon. Commander of the soldiers who carried out the massacre. Possibly, and if so ironically, uncle to the wife of MacIain's younger son. Died a bankrupt alcoholic in Bruges in 1696.

**Corrag.** Her name translates "finger" and this real witch used hers to cast spells. She was reputedly offered a Christian burial on Munda's Isle but a storm made it impossible to launch the boat.

**Hamilton,** Lieutenant-Colonel James. Deputy Governor of Fort William. Planned and ordered the massacre. Disappears from the record soon after.

**Hill,** Colonel Sir John. Parliamentary veteran of the English Civil War. First Military Governor of Fort William. Cleared of responsibility for the massacre. Retired to England in 1698.

**MacDonald,** Alasdair. Also known as MacIain after Iain MacDonald, the first chief of Glencoe MacDonalds. Alasdair was the twelfth chief. He was educated in France and was the prime target of the massacre, shot in back of head whilst dressing.

**MacDonald,** John. Escaped the massacre and succeeded his father as thirteenth chief.

**MacKay,** General Hugh of Scourie. Gaelic-speaking Highlander. Landed with William at Torbay and commanded his troops at Killiekrankie. Killed in 1692, along with most of his men, leading the Scots Brigade against the French at Steinkirk. Reputed last words were, "I am not happy about these orders."

**Stuart,** James. King (II) of England and (VII) of Scotland. Remained a refugee in Paris, combining writing theology with gross marital infidelity until his death in 1701. His son tried to regain the throne in 1715 as "The Old Pretender" and his grandson did the same in 1745 as "The Young Pretender", better known as Bonnie Prince Charlie. Both failed.

**William,** Prince of Orange (part of present day Netherlands) and King (III) of England and (II) of Scotland. Died in 1702, following an accident when his horse stumbled on a mole hill, resulting in the Jacobite toast "to the little gentleman in black velvet."

**The Soldiers:** Many of Argyll's men died in their first battle, in July 1693, at Doittignies. Although outnumbered 30:1 as they marched on the French, they still captured the enemy positions. Inevitably, the losses were severe, leaving the regiment unable to fight for two more years. It was disbanded in 1697.

# Acknowledgements

It is almost impossible to write about Glencoe without mentioning **John Prebble**. His books on the Highlands are among the most readable and informative available.

Another expert I'd like to thank is a man from Glencoe village itself, **Archie Kennedy**, President of the Pan Gaelic Association, who translated my Gaelic into something a Gaelic speaker would recognise.

My father-in-law, **Edmond Searing**, has once again demonstrated that retirement has not dulled his editing skills.

Ironically, I'd like to thank the half dozen publishers who rejected the original draft, especially the one who advised me to rewrite the whole thing and offer it to someone else. I did so. Dozens of people, aged from 8 to 80, read the manuscript and a much improved final copy resulted from their feedback. Thanks you all.

The illustrators did a remarkable job, especially as they were only aged between 11 and 15. It was a great help to have the backing of **Anita Reardon**, Head of Fine Art at Thomas Keble School, Eastcombe, **Caroline Harrison**, English teacher at Marling School Stroud, **Jo Grills**, Headteacher of Stroud Girls' High School and **Pat Savage**, Art teacher at

School of the Lion. Thanks to the members of Chalford Baptist Church who were used as models for the artists. You made superb rogues. In no picture did Christina's full face appear. We all have our own understanding of beauty so the artists left it all to the readers' imaginations. Another good reason for not showing her face was that the model was our lodger, **Yuko Tamura**. Her rich black hair was perfect but her Japanese face didn't quite suit the part.

Two outstanding artists are **Bill Young**, now retired, and Thomas Keble pupil, **Tara Moore**. Despite an age gap of 70 years between them, and the pair never having met, their joint effort produced the beautiful painting used for the cover of this book.

Finally, I'd like to dedicate this book to the two Mrs. Hobbs in my life. No, I'm not a bigamist.

The first is **Milly Hobbs**, my mum. Neither of us could have guessed, Mum, when you helped me draw a family tree for my homework, (thirty seven years ago!) that it would spark of research that would one day result in a book.

The second is person is **Yvonne Hobbs**, my wife, Manager of Centre Christian bookshop in Stroud. You are the most remarkable woman I've ever met and it was with a real sense of joy that this book came out just after we celebrated our Silver Wedding. If anyone wants to know how a wife can make a success of her marriage vows, they need look no further than you.